PENSION FOR MURDER

A BREEZE VILLAGE COZY MYSTERY

KATE MACLEAN

For Papa, who has taught me so much about writing and about living. And for Mom, without whose gentle push I never would have finished this book.

CHAPTER 1

"Your kitchen's on fire again," Lawrence strode from the kitchen into Virginia's cramped living room. Her friend gave her a chastising look. "What happened to your smoke detector?"

"The TV remote needed batteries. Did you put it out?" Virginia crossed the room. Flustered, she weaved between the aged furniture and stepped into her kitchen. Hazy light filtered in through a small window, illuminating the smoke-filled space.

"I turned the oven off," Lawrence said, stepping between Virginia and her ancient oven. "It'll put itself out. Don't open the oven door, that'll just give it more oxygen and make it worse."

"If this fire destroys my oven—"

"If this fire destroys that oven, I'll eat my hat." Lawrence chuckled and shook his head. The oven was an old Tappan electric, complete with a plate warming shelf perched above the range. Virginia's mother had installed it herself in the early sixties, and the beautiful turquoise appliance had seen more than its fair share of accidents and abuse.

Virginia watched through the small oven door, barely able to see the burning cake through the soot- and grime-covered glass.

"You ought to clean that," Lawrence said, bending over beside her to peer through the window.

"You ought to shut your damn mouth," Virginia retorted with half a smile, straightening up and pulling a glass from the wooden cabinet behind them. She opened the refrigerator, an off-white appliance from the nineties that looked downright modern in Virginia's museum of a kitchen, and pulled out a bottle of white grape juice.

"It's probably for the best anyway," she said, gesturing to the oven. "The doctors keep telling me not to eat so many sweets."

"Do you know how much sugar is in that juice?" Lawrence asked, raising one of his perfectly pruned eyebrows and nodding at the bottle in Virginia's hand.

"Well, I keep telling the doctors that past a certain age, you've got to take all the pleasures you can get in life. So if it's grape juice that does me in after all these years, that's just fine with me."

Virginia's cell phone played a tune and vibrated on the linoleum countertop. She looked at the screen, grimaced, then returned her attention to Lawrence.

"Anyway, this juice says it's made with one hundred percent real fruit."

"One hundred percent real fruit still has a lot of one hundred percent real sugar," Lawrence said. "Is that your children who have been trying to reach you all morning?"

Virginia shot Lawrence a perturbed look. "What's that got to do with anything?"

"It's your eightieth birthday, Virginia," Lawrence said gently. "They want to be part of your day, to celebrate you."

"They can celebrate me any day they want. Today they want to celebrate me turning another year older, and this birthday comes with a nice round number that they'll just wield as ammunition in their perpetual battle to push me into a retirement home." Virginia screwed up her face and, in a silly voice, said, "'But, Mom, you're *eighty* now.'" She drew out the word *eighty*, shaking her head and pursing her lips. "Today is my birthday, and if I don't want to hear a litany of reasons I should give up my home and independence, I don't have to."

At that moment, the doorbell rang, and Virginia set her glass down. "Keep an eye on the oven, will you? That's got to be Marney at the door."

Virginia pulled open the door to reveal not her best friend Marney but her two children. She started to swing the door shut, but Lucy stuck a blush-colored heel in the doorway, propping it open.

"Happy birthday, Mom!" she cooed, wrapping Virginia in a hug with one arm, the other arm outstretched and clinging to a bundle of outrageous balloons. Two of the balloons formed the numbers 8 and 0, while the others were all shaped like candles.

"Happy birthday," Jack echoed, stepping inside without waiting for an invitation. "Why does it smell like smoke in here?" He peered into the kitchen with narrowed eyes.

"Don't worry, just a minor incident with the cake,"

Lawrence said, stepping out of the kitchen and wrapping Lucy in a hug. While Lucy and Lawrence tied the balloons to the dining room chairs, Jack hurried into the kitchen.

"Isn't this the second fire this year?" he asked.

"Well, it's been a chaotic morning," Virginia responded, gesturing around, "what with Lawrence bustling around and my phone ringing off the hook with calls from you two."

"None of which you answered," Jack said. "And what's your excuse for the last fire? You were home alone, if I remember correctly."

Ignoring the conflict, Lucy went to the fridge and inspected its contents before pulling out a bottle of sparkling wine. "How long has this been in here?" she asked, frowning.

"Probably since the last time you all came over unannounced."

"Mom, I'm just saying maybe it's time to think about getting some help," Jack continued. "If you really don't want to move, there are in-home care aids we can look into. You *are* eighty, after all, and I just think—"

Virginia interrupted him with a dark laugh. "What did I tell you?" she asked Lawrence. "'You *are* eighty,'" she repeated, mocking her son. Virginia narrowed her eyes and frowned at Jack. "What I *am* is perfectly capable of living on my own. I have a system!" Virginia gestured around, and Jack's and Lucy's eyes grew wide as they noticed for the first time the small blue squares stuck to Virginia's appliances and doors. The little sticky notes contained reminders to turn off and unplug appliances, lock doors and windows before leaving the house, take the trash out on Tuesday and Friday.

Before either of her kids could survey her "system" more closely, Virginia's doorbell rang and the door swung open.

"I brought booze!" A woman in her mid-thirties wearing paint-covered overalls and a messy ponytail strode through the door, bags on her arms and a grin on her face. Virginia gave her daughter-in-law, Stephanie, a slight smile. "And look who else is here!"

Stephanie moved aside to reveal Marney approaching the stoop, carrying a cake. The top of the cake was hardly visible for the field of candles protruding from it, and everyone but Virginia's face lit up when they saw it.

"How'd you know we'd need a backup cake?" Lawrence asked with a laugh, taking the cake from Marney's hands and carrying it into the kitchen, where Lucy was opening windows in an attempt to fan the smoke from the room.

"When you're friends for this long, you just know," Marney said, eyes glittering. "Happy birthday, Virginia." She wrapped her dear friend in a tight hug.

"You didn't have to do that," Virginia said, a lump forming in her stomach. *Am I really so clumsy that Marney knew I'd need a backup cake? Maybe Lawrence sent her a text, and Marney's playing it up like she knew in advance?*

Virginia walked over to where Lawrence had set the cake on the counter. Homemade German chocolate. Virginia knew Marney always baked her cakes the night before and frosted them in the morning. *So she* did *know.*

"That's what friends are for! We help when we don't

have to, and we know each other well enough to offer help without being asked."

"I wish you'd stop offering," Virginia snapped before she could stop herself. Heat rushed to her face as her cheeks flushed with embarrassment. "I'm sorry," she said softly, "but I'm fine on my own, and I don't need as much help as you all seem to think I do."

"But you *did* need a backup cake," Marney said with a smile, ignoring Virginia's outburst.

As Stephanie opened kitchen drawers hunting for a lighter to light the candles, Jack walked over to where he'd set his briefcase by the front door and came back carrying a large three-ring binder. Virginia furrowed her brow.

"What's this?" she asked.

"Mom, I know we've brought this up before, and I know you've said you won't move, but—"

"But nothing," Virginia snapped. "I'm not going anywhere. End of story."

"We just thought if you had all the information in one place, so it wouldn't be too overwhelming…." Lucy took the binder from Jack's hands and started flipping through it. She held it up to show Virginia one of the pages, but Virginia shook her head and put her hand up to stop her.

"I've told you all before how I feel about this. I also told you I didn't want a big family birthday celebration. It's clear you don't care how or where I want to spend my time, and now I'm going to have to ask you to leave."

Virginia stepped to the side and gestured to the front door, her kids staring at her with wide eyes. "Go on," she said, nodding to the door.

"Mom, you can't be serious," Lucy said, a piece of her

perfectly curled blond hair falling in front of her furrowed brow.

"I love you, but I need you to respect my boundaries," Virginia said. Both Jack and Lucy looked shocked, while Stephanie wore a sad but understanding expression and gave a small nod. "Now, if you could please see yourselves out, and keep this in mind next time you think to hand me a three-inch binder on local nursing homes."

"Retirement communities," Jack said, unable to keep from correcting her even as he picked up his briefcase and opened the door.

As the door swung inward, Virginia saw a yellow piece of paper taped to the door. Though she couldn't make out what it said, her stomach clenched, and she snatched it off the door before either of her kids could see what it was. No matter what it turned out to be, she didn't want to give Jack another opportunity to insert himself into her life, trying to solve her problems. So when Jack shot her a puzzled look, she shrugged and said, "Roofing company's been coming around taping fliers to everyone's doors. Damn nuisance, it is!"

She folded the paper, and after she'd hugged her children and sent them on their way, she tucked it underneath a book on the long, narrow table that ran the length of her dining room wall. For Virginia's entire childhood, her mother would line up all the dishes on this table, and they'd walk past one by one serving food onto their plates before sitting down at the dining room table for dinner together. In the good years, there would be plates of ham with beautifully darkened skin, scalloped potatoes, green beans, freshly baked bread, cheese, and always dessert.

Even when Daddy was out of work and money was tight, Mother worked magic in that tiny kitchen and laid out the results along that long table every night.

Now, the table contained unopened mail and back issues of magazines, and Virginia ate Hamburger Helper more nights than she'd admit. She never did share her mother's skill or love for cooking.

Neither Marney nor Lawrence commented on the yellow slip of paper. Instead, the three ate Marney's German chocolate cake and made stiff conversation about Dorothea from down the street robbing the cradle with her new boyfriend. When they'd finished their cake, Marney pulled out a deck of cards, but Virginia shook her head.

"Not today," she said, and the two understood and took their leave.

When she was again alone in her home, the smell of smoke still lingering on her yellowed lace curtains, Virginia pulled the piece of paper from underneath the book. She couldn't make out the smaller text, but, holding it close to her face, she could clearly see, in all capital letters across the top, *NOTICE OF INTENT TO FORE-CLOSE*. In slightly smaller lettering underneath, it read, *YOU MAY LOSE YOUR PROPERTY.*

irginia's heart sank and her stomach twisted. Her eyes strained in vain to make out the rest of the document. She crossed from the dining room into the adjacent living room, where its large window overlooked the backyard, letting in more light. As she searched for her reading glasses, her mind flicked back to the stacks of unopened mail on the buffet table in the dining room. How many of those could have been bills? Sure, she might have forgotten something, but the mortgage was paid. How could she be about to lose her home?

Her fingers found her reading glasses in the bottom of her purse among mini candy bars, pads of sticky notes, and pens advertising various businesses around Seaview. Virginia donned the glasses and held the bright yellow paper up so she could read it.

"A tax lien," she read aloud, "in the amount of $9,673?" The color drained from Virginia's face, and she pulled the paper closer, her eyes fixed on the figure.

She'd been paying her taxes, hadn't she?

The notice instructed Virginia to contact the claimant and pay the lien to avoid foreclosure but didn't list a deadline. *If you want me to pay you ten grand to keep my house, the least you could do is tell me when you need it by.* She felt the tight burning of tears coming to her eyes as she bit back her panic.

Virginia dug again through her purse, this time pulling out her checkbook and flipping quickly to the back. The balance sheet showed she had $5,244 in her checking account, but the last entry was from three weeks ago, and Virginia knew she'd written a check at the pharmacy and deposited her Social Security check just the week before. *If Jack were here, I'd be getting a lesson on the importance of balancing my checkbook. No, if Jack were here, he'd take the checkbook out of my hands and get to work rectifying the situation himself as if I were a child, one who makes messes at every turn but is too incompetent to play any role in cleaning them up.*

Setting her checkbook on the side table, Virginia walked down the hall toward the bedroom, her slippers quiet on the old wooden floors. Lucy had bought her a runner for the hallway at Christmas, claiming she thought it would brighten the place up, but Virginia knew her concern was the slickness of the smooth, worn wood. When Virginia had insisted she liked the floors as they were, Lucy had settled for giving her mom slippers with little circular grip pads on the bottom. Virginia had balked, but after one embarrassing fall, thankfully with no serious consequences, she'd taken to wearing them and lying to herself that it was to keep her feet warm and not to prevent future falls.

Kneeling beside her bed, Virginia leaned into the bedframe, sliding it along the floor on its furniture-pad-covered feet. With the bed pushed aside, Virginia took a deep breath and pressed on the floorboards one by one. Nothing, nothing. Then there it was. *Creak.*

Heart pounding, she lifted the board and pulled out a canvas bag, dumping its contents onto the bed.

"Twenty, forty, sixty..." she counted the bills, stacking them neatly as she went. What seemed like a mountain of bills quickly became neat little stacks, and when she was finished, Virginia had counted out a measly $3,000. She wobbled on her feet, and as her heartbeat drummed in her ears, Virginia found herself twirling her engagement ring on her left hand the way she always did when she was worried.

She pulled the ring from her finger, twisting it back and forth to get it over her knuckle, which in her old age no longer straightened completely. In the light, the diamond sparkled, and Virginia remembered the afternoon when Earl had given it to her.

The two of them, twenty years old and full of optimism, had taken kayaks out on the water and planned to explore Little Ogulla Island. The waves had been rougher than they'd imagined, but Earl didn't want to turn back, and Virginia had felt so alive, the sun shining down on her hair, long and blond then, and the sea breeze blowing the wide linen sleeves of her shirt. When Earl's kayak flipped, Virginia screamed, and then when he bobbed to the surface and spit a stream of saltwater at her, she laughed so hard she flipped her own kayak. As the two of them treaded water, laughing too hard to right their boats, a dolphin swam by, almost close enough to touch.

Now, alone in her bedroom, Virginia examined the ring, then pushed it back onto her finger.

"No," she said aloud. "There's got to be another way."

* * *

THE SMALL CLUTCH purse glimmered in the dim closet light as Virginia held it aloft, its intricate black beading flashing subtly as she turned the bag in her hands. Virginia checked the inside for a tag, a logo, some indication of the bag's value, but found nothing.

"It's vintage," she muttered to herself, thinking of the three new thrift stores that had appeared on the downtown strip in the last year alone, wondering whether anything she had would be considered cool or desirable by today's youth.

She set the black beaded clutch aside and pulled a fur coat from the back of the closet. She'd bought it to wear to the celebratory dinner after Earl defended his thesis and officially became Dr. Walker. A chemist, he'd always been the smart one. So dedicated.

Into the pile it went.

On top of the beaded black clutch and fur coat went more handbags, more coats, some jewelry her Aunt Agnes had given her that she'd always found a bit gauche, and a pair of heels her swollen, twisted feet hadn't allowed her to wear in decades.

Virginia assessed the pile, wondering how much it must be worth.

She looked down to see what had sent her flying and saw the binder Jack and Lucy had given her sitting on the floor. She cursed under her breath, then picked up the binder and brought it closer. Jack had printed the words *Retirement Communities and Care Options* on the cover in big black block letters. Inside, the binder was full, nearly to bursting, with pages printed and housed in clear plastic sheets. A table of contents listed all the retirement homes and senior living communities in a fifty-mile radius, as well as a variety of in-home care options.

She flipped through the book, turning the slick plastic-covered sheets to reveal photographs of smiling gray-haired men and women seated around round tables, prim nurses standing to the side. For each facility, Jack included activity calendars and reviews from residents and their children. As Virginia turned page after page to reveal picture after picture of smiling seniors, Virginia felt the walls closing in on her. Suddenly the floral wallpaper she'd always loved seemed worn, and the blue sticky notes seemed less like friendly reminders and more like taunting bits of proof that she couldn't take care of herself.

In anger, Virginia slammed the book shut, then threw it at the wall, crying out in pain and cradling her injured wrist. A blue sticky note fell to the floor, its flimsy hold shaken by the impact, and Virginia struggled over to pick it up and return it to its place.

The next morning, Virginia lifted herself out of bed, wincing as her wrist reminded her of the previous evening's fall. She clenched her fist and tried to wiggle her wrist front to back, side to side. Pain shot through her arm with the movement.

Wrapped in a robe, Virginia crossed her yard to knock on Lawrence's front door with her uninjured hand. The bright red door stood out against the pale yellow siding, and a St. Patrick's Day-themed wreath hung at head height. Soon, Virginia knew, it would be replaced by pastel flowers and little painted wooden eggs for Easter, and then bright sunflowers for the summer before a red, white, and blue wreath took its place.

The door swung back to reveal Lawrence standing in the doorway wearing a black tracksuit with red and white stripes up the sides. The chest was emblazoned with a seagull wielding a bowling ball, its wings ending in feathered fingers.

"Nice getup," Virginia said, looking him up and down.

Lawrence gave her a small smile. "Bowling match later today. If we keep up our winning streak, the Seaview Seagulls are on our way to the championships. What do you need?"

Virginia bristled at the insinuation that she was only there because she needed something, mostly because it was true.

"Can you drive me to the doctor's office?" she asked. "I tripped last night and hurt my wrist." She held up her right arm, showing the swollen joint where her forearm met her wrinkled hand.

Lawrence's eyes got wide, and his mouth dropped in concern. "Yeah, sure," he said, looking around. "Let me call Barry and let him know I can't make the match. Jeez, Virginia, do you think it's broken? If it's so bad you can't drive, it might be."

Virginia winced. "I think I could drive," she said softly, "but the forecast says it's going to rain."

At this, Lawrence straightened, his tall form still muscular in old age. "Virginia," he said firmly, "there is a fifteen percent chance of rain today."

Virginia looked up at him, eyes wet. *Please don't make me say it.*

Thankfully, Lawrence just sighed and picked up his keys from the small silver dish that sat on his entryway table under a round mirror. He took a quick glance at his appearance, running his fingers over his eyebrows and pulling his shoulders back, flashing a bright smile that contrasted handsomely with his dark skin.

"All right," he sighed. "Let's go."

The doctor's office was on the third floor of a stucco

building plopped right in the middle of a residential neighborhood. The building hosted an eclectic array of tenants: a beauty school, a photography studio, a cycle bar that attracted fit, young clientele, and Virginia's doctor's office, which attracted old, sick clientele.

Dr. DiMarco had been in this office space for longer than any other tenants. The carpeting in the waiting room was a dark tan, thick and plush, a relic of another time. On the walls hung abstract art reminiscent of the works of Jackson Pollock, and behind the reception desk stood rows and rows of accordion shelving filled with files dating back decades.

"Virginia," Dr. DiMarco said with a smile, coming out from behind the desk to shake her hand. "What brings you in today?"

Dr. DiMarco had been Virginia's primary care physician for thirty years. She'd started coming to his office when he was a brand new medical doctor, striking out on his own, eager to establish his own practice. Now, in place of the young, spry man with olive skin and dark, wavy hair, stood a slightly-stooped, weathered man whose hair had long ago turned white but whose eyes still glimmered with enthusiasm for life.

Virginia held up her arm so he could see it. "I took a fall last night."

Dr. DiMarco eyed her wrist, nodded, then went back behind the dark wooden desk to glance at the screen of an ancient computer. "I have an opening until eleven. Let's go take a look."

Lawrence made himself comfortable in the waiting room, flipping through an old issue of *Better Homes and*

Gardens, while Virginia followed Dr. DiMarco back to one of three exam rooms. Virginia sat on the table, paper crinkling underneath her, and Dr. DiMarco took her arm in his hands. He probed at her wrist and asked her to demonstrate her range of motion with it.

"FOOSH," he said, and Virginia looked at him quizzically. "Fall On Outstretched Hand." He nodded and looked at Virginia. "It's one of the most common injuries we see in folks our age." Virginia knew Dr. DiMarco was a dozen years younger than she, if not more, but appreciated the remark. "Let's take a few X-rays, shall we, and see if there's a fracture."

Virginia's wrist was not fractured, merely sprained, and she emerged from the exam room with a brace on her wrist. She dug in her purse as she crossed the waiting room and felt her stomach sink when her fingers didn't come into contact with her checkbook. "Drat," she muttered to herself before looking up and offering an apologetic smile to Dr. DiMarco behind the desk. "I left my checkbook on the table in my living room."

Before she could propose to Dr. DiMarco that she run home and come back to pay him that afternoon, Lawrence had pulled his wallet from his pocket and handed the doctor a sleek black card. "I've got it."

Virginia's face flushed at his generosity.

As she averted her eyes, she noticed a small corkboard on the wall by the door. A handful of brochures and advertisements for local chiropractors and specialists, pharmacies, and fitness classes hung on it. In the center of the board hung a notice on the doctor's office letterhead that said, in big letters, *Assistant Wanted.* While Lawrence settled the bill with the doctor, Virginia pulled her pad of sticky notes from her purse and wrote on the top of the stack, *Job—Assistant.* She dropped the note back into her bag as Lawrence joined her, then wrapped her arm around his and let him lead her from the office.

* * *

"Do you want to get some lunch?" Lawrence asked, turning the key in the ignition of the Lincoln Town Car he treated like his baby and turning to Virginia in the passenger seat. It was just starting to sprinkle, and Virginia was glad she hadn't tried to drive herself. The first hint of rain set her anxiety on edge, and she'd have sat in her car in the parking lot waiting for it to stop before she could drive herself home. "I already told the guys I'd miss today's match, so I've got a free afternoon. We can go to Miss B's."

At the mention of Miss B's, Virginia's mouth watered and her stomach rumbled, voicing its excitement at the suggestion. "If you're buying," Virginia said with a laugh.

Even on a Monday, parking near Miss B's was a nightmare. Lawrence parked two blocks away, and the two walked in the drizzle to the legendary fried chicken establishment. A whitewashed brick building with green and white striped awnings, the restaurant was squeezed between a used bookstore and a tobacco shop. Virginia thought both seemed to have benefited from the presence of Miss B's. Once rundown, both businesses sported new awnings above their doors and fresh signs displaying their names.

A bell jangled as Lawrence pressed open the door and held it for Virginia. Inside, the restaurant was warm and lively, and the sound of chicken frying in cast iron sizzled through the small dining room. The bright white linoleum floors and canary yellow booths stood out against the walls, which were covered in photographs patrons stapled up during their visits. Happy customers smiled out from the photos, including several celebrities and politicians.

"Inside or outside?" a waitress asked, flashing a smile that looked genuine despite the sweat on her brow. "We just opened our covered patio for the spring."

"Outside would be lovely," Lawrence said, returning the smile. Virginia thought she saw the waitress flush and her smile deepen, and thought only Lawrence could woo twenty-year-old women at age seventy. The man certainly hadn't lost an ounce of charm since he'd aged.

The two followed the waitress outside and settled into mismatched chairs around a wrought-iron table. The drizzle bounced off the tin roof of the patio which protruded from the back of the restaurant. Their water glasses tottered on the uneven surface.

"Springtime in the south," Lawrence said appreciatively.

By the time she and Lawrence had cleaned their plates —crispy fried chicken, candied yams, and fried okra— Virginia felt lighter despite the heavy lunch. The breeze, the smell of rain and azaleas blooming, the laughter and chatter and culinary experience had caused her to all but forget her predicament. It wasn't until she'd fastened her seatbelt back in Lawrence's car and reached into her purse for a mint that she found the note reminding her of the open secretary position and remembered her dire circumstances. She needed money, and she needed it now.

After bidding Lawrence adieu and crossing the threshold into her living room, Virginia dropped her bag and walked to her fridge, where she'd stuck a list of important phone numbers on the front. She dialed the number for the doctor's office.

"Dr. DiMarco," she said nervously, "it's Virginia."

"Is everything all right?" he asked. "I'll be right with you," she could hear him say to another patient.

"It is. Actually, I noticed that you're looking for an assistant, and I wondered if I could help."

There was silence on the other end of the line.

"Well, you're right that I need an assistant, but I was hoping to find someone with…" Dr. DiMarco trailed off and Virginia filled in the rest in her mind. Someone younger, she knew. As the silence between them grew, Dr. DiMarco cleared his throat. "I really need someone to help me modernize the practice a bit. Someone with experience with the latest billing and scheduling software."

"I understand," Virginia choked out, her voice cracking.

She hadn't realized that she'd already begun subconsciously envisioning herself as a career woman once again, depositing paychecks and solving her own problems. As that vision abruptly came crashing down, she felt lost, the reality of her situation sinking in. She was going to have to tell her kids. What would Jack say when she told him she'd forgotten to pay her property taxes for so long she was losing her home? And Lucy? She'd never said as much, but Virginia knew Lucy was as emotionally attached to the family home as Virginia herself was.

After a pause so long Virginia thought maybe the doctor had hung up, his voice came through, quieter. "But if you really want the job, I guess we could give it a try." His voice had compassion in it, like he could sense Virginia's desperation. "Can you start on Friday?"

CHAPTER 4

"You're late," Marney said with a sly smile, looking up from her menu across the laminate table where Virginia had just sat down.

"Fashionably," Virginia said with a shrug.

Marney wore light pink lipstick and small pearl earrings, her wispy gray hair curled neatly atop her head. Rhinestones adorned the collar of her white t-shirt, and her neatly pedicured toes poked out of a pair of sparkly sandals beneath her coral linen capris. As long as Virginia had known her, Marney had always been neatly put-together. Subdued. Virginia thought if Marney dressed the way she truly desired, she'd probably be wearing feather boas and sequins day in and day out. But Marney had always opted for less attention-grabbing styles as if her abusive ex-husband Dean could sense feathers from however many hundreds of miles away she'd left him, like she always had to be hiding.

"I ordered us each a Bloody Mary," Marney said, picking the menu back up and blocking her face from

Virginia's view. "And I'm thinking of trying their new crab cake sandwich."

Virginia picked up her own menu. Bo's Biscuits was the latest incarnation of what she, Marney, and Lawrence had always just called "the place on the corner." The small brick building had been a restaurant as long as they could remember, but never one place for longer than two or three years. And though every restaurant so far had failed, it was never long before another took its place on the corner of First and Seymore. Bo's was a hip brunch establishment that specialized in homemade biscuits. Neon lights and bright paintings by local artists adorned the exposed brick walls. The restaurant's primary clientele was much younger than Virginia and Marney, and the other booths and tables were occupied by people in their twenties with tattoos, piercings, and brightly colored hair.

"What's with the wrist brace?" Marney asked, eyeing the brace as Virginia tried to choose between biscuits and gravy or a waffle.

"Oh, nothing much. Just gave it a little twist the other night."

Marney narrowed her eyes but didn't push the subject. Instead, she said, "I have some news for you."

Virginia folded her menu and placed it back on the table, looking warily across at her friend.

Marney took a deep breath, opened her mouth to speak, then closed it again. She looked down at her hands, folded on the table in front of her, then looked back up at Virginia. Finally, she said, "I'm moving."

Virginia fixed her eyes on Marney but said nothing.

"To Breeze Village," Marney added.

"Is this a joke?" Virginia asked, louder than she intended. "Did Jack put you up to this?"

"I didn't know how to tell you," Marney said, reaching across the table to take Virginia's soft hand in her own, but Virginia jerked away.

"What do you mean, you didn't know how to tell me? How long have you been waiting?"

"I… A while. I'm moving tomorrow." Marney lowered her eyes as Virginia's jaw dropped. She opened it to respond but, not finding the words, closed it again. "Into one of their independent living cottages. I've been eyeing them for a while. One of them just came available, and, well, I'm really excited about it."

"So excited about it you didn't mention it to your best friend?"

"I knew you'd be upset!"

"You're damn right I'm upset!"

An uncomfortable server approached their table with two Bloody Marys in his hands.

"Excuse me," he stuttered, setting the drinks in front of the pair. "Are you ready to order?"

Marney turned to him and gave him a beaming smile as if nothing were amiss at their table. "I think we'll need another minute or two, please," she said, sending him away. She turned back to Virginia, the smile falling from her face. "You know I've been feeling like my house is too big. Dylan has to come over and help me clean the place every few weeks, and I've started hiring a neighborhood boy to do my lawn. It's just too much for me. These cottages, Virginia, they really are darling. The perfect little size, and no lawn to tend, and I can eat in the

Breeze Village dining room so I don't have to cook, and—"

"And why not tell your best friend of almost fifty years that you've decided to move?" Virginia cut her off, standing up. "That's low, Marney," she spat, turning on her heel and leaving the restaurant, the server watching wide-eyed as she left.

Virginia half expected Marney to follow her out of the restaurant, to apologize for keeping such a big secret. Instead, she reached her car alone and, fuming, began to cry.

* * *

"Did you know?" Virginia shouted in between knocks at Lawrence's door. "Did she tell you?"

The door swung open and Lawrence pulled Virginia inside, looking around to see neighbors poking their heads out of their homes at the commotion. "What is the matter with you?" he hissed.

"Marney just gave me some news," Virginia said, voice hard. Lawrence's face fell, and his eyes avoided Virginia's. "I knew you knew. And you didn't say anything to me?" She raised her voice again with the accusation. Though she'd suspected he'd known, the confirmation stung deeply, and her voice shook as tears sprung up in her eyes.

"It wasn't my news to tell." Lawrence held his hands up in a gesture of surrender. "I told her she should tell you back when she was first considering it."

"But she didn't. And you didn't, either." Virginia's chest heaved with anger, and she wobbled before grabbing the back of a chair to steady herself. She mentally ran through the list of people Marney would have told. "Dylan knows, of course. She'll have known longer than anyone." Her eyes widened. "Do Jack and Lucy know?" She looked up at Lawrence, a pleading look on her face, and he gave a small, apologetic nod.

"I really am the last to know." Her voice was soft but cold, and her expression hardened.

"Virginia," Lawrence protested, but Virginia was already out the door and striding as quickly as she could manage across the lawn to her own house. She slammed the door so hard the pictures on her wall shook, and she hoped Lawrence could hear it from next door.

Inside, Virginia's stomach churned, her face flushed. She wanted to rage, scream, and bang her fists into the walls, but after one feeble swing with her good hand, she leaned her forehead against the wall, supporting herself as the tears began to fall. She should have been the one to go visit apartments with Marney. She should have been the one helping her pack, reassuring her when Marney's anxiety inevitably flared up at the impending change. Instead, she was the last to know.

She felt shame as she realized part of the reason she felt so angry was that she was always the one spreading news in their neighborhood. If it hadn't been so personally devastating, Marney's moving from the Grove Park neighborhood into Breeze Village after decades would make for amazing gossip. If Marney was moving, who would be next? Virginia could hear the whispers now.

Collecting herself, she picked up her phone. She might be the last to know in their inner circle, but she still had a

was mistaken. Will you be at the neighborhood tea party in two weeks? It's here at my house this time, and I'm just so excited to have everyone over!"

"Yes, I'll be there." Of course, Virginia had forgotten the gathering, but she knew it was on the calendar by her bedside. She'd see it and be reminded, and she'd show up and smile at the circle of neighbors who had all known before Virginia that her best friend was moving.

CHAPTER 5

A knock at Virginia's door interrupted her silent battle with her bladder. She had been tossing and turning for an hour, trying to find a comfortable position that didn't put pressure on her abdomen so she could sulk in bed just a little longer.

"Just a minute!" she called, throwing her legs over the side of the bed, sliding her feet into her slippers, and shuffling into the bathroom. Before she could emerge, wrapped in her old plush robe, she heard the lock turn and the door open. "Shit," she muttered. If the visitor had a key, it was either Lawrence, Marney, or her kids, none of whom she wanted to see that morning.

"It's me," Lawrence's voice boomed through her house.

"I'm not home," Virginia called feebly.

"You're hilarious," he said when she turned from the hallway into the living room. He held up a brown paper bag and nodded to the two cups of steaming coffee he'd set on the side table. Her stomach sinking, Virginia saw her checkbook was still there and walked over and put it in her purse. "I brought breakfast," Lawrence said.

"I already ate," Virginia lied. "I have a busy day planned, so I don't really have time for a visit."

"You haven't already eaten. You've been in bed. You're out of coffee beans, by the way—I checked—so don't tell me you're going to make coffee on your own." He strode from the living room into the kitchen, weaving through the cramped dining room where the gold helium balloons still bobbed, tied to the chair backs, and pulled two plates from her cabinets before digging into the paper bag and pulling out a croissant. "Ham and cheese stuffed," he said, setting the flaky pastry on one plate and pushing it toward her.

Virginia accepted it reluctantly and took a bite. Her eyes rolled back into her head, and she wished she could pretend it wasn't delicious.

"Why are you here?" she asked instead.

"We have a busy day, like you said, and I wanted to make sure you fueled appropriately."

"We?" Virginia asked, confused.

"We're going to help Marney move into her cottage at Breeze Village."

"No." Virginia set the rest of her pastry down on the plate, shaking her head. "I am not going."

"Virginia," Lawrence insisted, his brown eyes drilling into Virginia's gray-blue ones.

"Marney kept this from me until yesterday. Now you're trying to make me go help her?"

"I'm not going to make you. But you're Marney's best friend. You've known her for nearly fifty years, and she needs you today. She's excited, but she's scared, and you know she feels horrible for keeping this from you. Your support means everything to her, and you're going to give it to her today."

Virginia mulled over Lawrence's words while she chewed the last bite of savory croissant.

"I don't want to," she said, knowing she sounded like a petulant child.

"And yet, you're going to do it, anyway. How gracious of you." He smiled at her, and she knew he was right.

BREEZE VILLAGE RETIREMENT Community sat on the corner of Marsh Point Drive and Johnston Street, not quite fifteen minutes from Virginia's house, in an old neighborhood filled with live oaks dripping Spanish moss. Breeze Village was comprised of one large main U-shaped building and ten little cottages around the back. All the buildings had pale blue siding and bright white shutters and trim, and a courtyard stood between the main building and the cottages.

Two potted palm trees framed the front door, and a large porch hosted half a dozen rocking chairs and potted plants bursting with bright pink and yellow blooms. In one of the rocking chairs, a waif of a woman sat knitting, tubes running from her face down to a small oxygen tank on wheels. Virginia winced at the sight, then turned and followed Lawrence through the double doors into the main lobby.

Inside, the space felt like a cross between a hotel and a

hospital. The floors were shining tile and the distinct smell of antiseptic hung in the air, but the upholstered furniture and artwork adorning the walls looked suspiciously similar to that in the Holiday Inn across town. Behind a large curved reception desk sat a correspondingly large, bored-looking woman.

"Excuse me," Lawrence said, giving her his signature smile, "but we're here to visit a new resident, Marney Richards. Today is her first day here."

The woman smiled up at Lawrence, crinkles forming around her eyes, and looked down at the computer in front of her.

Before she could answer, Virginia heard a familiar voice. "You made the right choice, Mom." Virginia turned to see Marney and her daughter, Dylan, walking through the lobby. Marney was carrying a small statue of a black and white spotted dog, while Dylan had her arms laden with boxes labeled *Kitchen* and *Bedroom*.

At the sight of Virginia and Lawrence, Marney's already-beaming face lit up even more. "Visitors! I didn't expect to have company so soon!" She grinned at Virginia as if nothing had happened between them, then led them through the lobby.

Lawrence took one of the boxes from Dylan's arms and the three followed Marney from the lobby through a dining room filled with white cloth-covered round tables, then through one of three sets of French doors out onto the courtyard. A stone path wound from the concrete patio, dotted with dark green umbrellas and small tables and chairs, through the courtyard, lined on both sides with stunning gardens.

"There's a gardening club here," Marney said enthusiastically. "Virginia, you would love it!"

Virginia pursed her lips but didn't give a response.

They crossed the courtyard and turned left as Marney led them to the third cottage from the end.

"I think I'll have to hang a wreath on my door," Marney said. "Lawrence, I'll need your help with that! And Virginia, I was thinking of planting pansies in pots on either side of the door. Is it too late in the year for them?"

Dylan balanced her box on her knee to free up one hand and swing the door open. Though tiny, the inside of the cottage felt airy and open. Virginia found herself thinking that it was really quite cute, then quashed the thought as quickly as it had come. *No, Breeze Village is not cute. It's a place where people who can't handle living on their own anymore come to give up their last vestiges of independence.*

She looked around, taking in the space. Beige carpet covered most of the cottage floor, save for the kitchen and bathroom, which had white linoleum. The walls were a matching light beige, and Marney had already started propping up pieces of art against the walls where she planned to hang them.

"I think I'll probably paint it blue, or maybe yellow?" Marney said, looking around, eyes twinkling with excitement. "Definitely need to brighten the place up a little."

On the back wall, a large sliding glass door let natural light fill the open living and dining area, and only a bar-height counter separated the space from the kitchen. Two doors led off of the main room, one to the bedroom and one to the bathroom, connected via a walk-through closet that also housed a washer and dryer.

"I'm going to have to go shopping to fill this massive closet," Marney laughed.

Virginia hadn't seen her friend so bubbly with excitement since Dylan's high school graduation. Even when Dylan graduated from the police academy, Marney's excitement and pride had been tempered with worry. This was pure joy, and Virginia hated herself for wanting to be anywhere else in that moment.

"I'm going to make another run to the car," Dylan said and left, heading back across the courtyard.

"How would you two feel about a glass of iced tea?" Marney asked. "I think I saw a pitcher in the dining room on our way through."

From the dining room, Virginia could see a small office off the lobby and two activities rooms. Two hallways protruded from the lobby; Virginia could see down one, a line of identical white doors to residents' rooms, but the other was blocked by a large gray door with a sign indicating that an alarm would sound if it were opened. A card reader hung on the wall beside the door.

"That's the memory ward," Marney said. The alarmed wing of the building for residents with advanced stages of dementia to make sure they didn't wander off.

Virginia shuddered again. Of all her friends she thought might be first to move into a place like this, Virginia still couldn't believe it was Marney who was about to be calling Breeze Village home.

"I know it's unexpected," Marney said, "but I am feeling really good about this decision."

Lawrence nodded in agreement, and Virginia tried to plaster a smile on her face while she felt her throat constricting.

"How are you three doing today?" A nurse in pale pink scrubs approached their table, yanking Virginia from her thoughts. Her long false eyelashes fluttered as she blinked from Lawrence to Marney and then settled on Virginia. "I heard we have a new resident joining us today. Are you Marney?"

Virginia opened her mouth in surprise. "I most certainly am not." She gestured to the badge on her chest that read *Visitor.* "What kind of place is this, anyway, where the staff doesn't even know a resident from a visitor? Marney, are you sure you're making the right choice here?"

Marney, Lawrence, and the nurse were silent for a moment until Marney turned to Virginia and said quietly, "I think this was a mistake."

"That's what I'm trying to tell you." Virginia nodded vigorously.

"No, I mean your coming here. I think you should leave."

Virginia recoiled. "Are you serious?"

"It's clear you don't want to be here. Dylan and I can handle the unpacking ourselves."

Virginia remained seated until Lawrence stood up and kissed Marney on the top of her head. "Tell Dylan I said goodbye. I'll see you later." He turned to Virginia. "Let's go."

She followed him through the lobby, feeling like a small child who had just been disciplined in a department store as other shoppers looked on. When they turned in their visitors' badges at the front desk, Virginia asked the woman, "Do you have visitors' bathrooms?"

The receptionist nodded and pointed down the hall not blocked by the door with the card reader. "Halfway down that hallway, you'll see 'em. Men's on the left, women's on the right."

Virginia nodded and turned to Lawrence, who told her he'd wait in the car.

As she walked down the hallway, most of the residents' doors were closed. Some had decorations or cards from friends and family displayed. She passed the occasional open door, TV sounds drifting from the rooms. From one room, she heard Johnny Cash playing on the radio especially loudly. She rapped sharply on the doorframe and poked her head inside.

"Would you mind turning that down?" she asked the woman inside, who was sitting in a dark blue leather recliner facing an old radio opposite the door. "The entire hallway can hear it." The woman didn't respond, and Virginia started to back out of the room, embarrassed to have intruded, when she noticed the woman's head seemed to be slumped to the side.

"Excuse me, are you okay?" she asked, taking a cautious step closer.

The woman still didn't respond, and when Virginia took another step closer she saw why.

The woman was dead.

* * *

VIRGINIA RECOILED IN HORROR, crying out in surprise.

"Oh, my god," she said, softly, then louder. "Oh, my god. Can somebody help?"

Virginia backed out of the room and into the hallway, calling for help until the nurse with the pink scrubs and false eyelashes came running from the lobby, another staff member on her heels. Residents up and down the hall poked their heads from their rooms to see what was going on.

"I found her," Virginia said simply, looking back over to where the woman sat motionless in her chair. Her eyes were glassy and her mouth hung ajar.

The nurses checked for a pulse, but it was clear from the beginning there would be no pulse to find.

"Can you call it in?" the pink-clad nurse asked the other, who nodded and left the room. "You can come with me," she then said, turning to Virginia. "I'm Haley, by the way. Would you like a cup of tea?"

Virginia nodded but stood still as though rooted fast to the spot. She couldn't tear her eyes from the woman's pale face. Haley had closed the deceased's eyes, but her face was still contorted, and the radio playing in the background made the scene feel like a fever dream.

"You okay?" Haley asked, turning to see why Virginia wasn't with her. When she saw Virginia's horrified face, she softened. "Her name was Ruth," she said, glancing over at the body in the chair. "She's been here three years. This one's going to hurt." Her voice cracked and she cleared her throat, shaking her head. "But it's part of the job. I'm so sorry you had to be the one to find her."

Virginia lowered her gaze to the floor, ashamed to

have lashed out at this woman who was now comforting her.

Haley led Virginia to a corner of the dining room and handed her a styrofoam cup of hot tea, and Virginia took the string in hand and bobbed the tea bag up and down in the steaming water.

"Will I have to talk to the police now?" Virginia asked. "Since I found her?"

Haley's brow furrowed slightly. "The coroner should come, but I don't think the police will come. The coroner will issue the death certificate, and then the funeral home can come to remove the body. Ruth has a son, Matt—he visits all the time—so we'll call him and give him the news so he can make the arrangements with the funeral home."

"No police?"

"It's usually just the coroner unless there's something unusual or suspicious." Haley shrugged, and Virginia's stomach turned. She thought she might be sick.

Marney was moving into a place where people died.

People died everywhere, of course, and the nurse had said Ruth had been at Breeze Village for three years, so it's not like she moved in and immediately dropped dead, but what had once seemed like a vague and distant concern suddenly seemed real and pressing. And all around her, Breeze Village bustled on as usual. The residents who had poked their heads out to see what was the matter had all returned to their rooms. Card games had started up at several of the tables in the dining room, bringing uproarious laughter, accusations of cheating, and triumphant shouts. And twenty yards away, a woman lay dead in her chair, and nobody seemed to care.

CHAPTER 6

*V*irginia woke the next morning more tired than she'd been when she'd gone to sleep the night before. She'd tossed and turned and seen Ruth's contorted face in her dreams, then woke covered in sweat. Before the sun peaked above the horizon, she checked the weather forecast and drove down to the beach.

Though the town was called Seaview, Virginia had always felt that was a bit of a misnomer, seeing as the beach was a solid half-hour drive from town. Marshview would have been a more apt name. Still, the town was beautiful, and though Virginia had left briefly after school, thinking she was going to travel the world to find herself, it had become clear to her immediately that Seaview was where she was meant to be. She'd returned after six months and never left.

She parked her silver Honda at the north end of the beach and started down the sandy path through the trees. The March air was cool, and she wrapped her shawl around herself. On the horizon, the first rays of the morning sun were just coming into view. The waves roared as they broke on the shore.

Holding her sandals in her hand, Virginia made her way down to the wet sand, digging her toes down into it. As the waves rolled in, the cold water covered her feet and ankles, then receded, and Virginia timed her breaths to the tempo of the waves.

There was no one else at this end of the beach. Even once the sun had risen, Virginia knew there weren't likely to be many people up this way. It was her favorite spot, secluded and peaceful. She and Marney had spent so many mornings here, sharing their lives with one another. Their griefs, their losses, their successes, their fears. The struggles they'd faced in parenting, in marriage, in their careers. This was the spot where they came to bare their souls to one another, never letting each other carry a burden alone.

Virginia dropped her shawl from her shoulders, a shiver running through her, then slipped her sweatpants down to her ankles and removed her sweater and wrist brace, leaving only her swimsuit between her skin and the cool air. She never came to the beach without running into the water. It made her feel alive. Though it was barely fifty degrees, she took a deep breath and ran into the surf, gasping as the cold water hit her belly. Then, taking another gulp of air, she plugged her nose and dunked herself into the sea.

When she broke through the surface once again, she wore an exhilarated smile. She was still hurt by Marney's betrayal, still shaken by her confrontation with death, but she was also suddenly cold and wet and alone in the ocean, and the sensation of the water churning around her body had the effect of clearing her mind, of demanding she focus only on how she felt in that moment.

By the time Virginia toweled off and made it back to her car, her worries were concentrated less around her friend's loyalty or mortality and more around her capabilities as an assistant in a medical office. She'd spent her working years as a saleswoman at Dillard's, and though she felt she had a knack for helping customers find the right garments for their occasions, she wasn't sure she'd acquired many transferable skills.

As her internal monologue enumerated the ways in which she might bungle her first day, she turned up the radio to drown it out. The Eagles sang through her speakers, and she sang along and let them carry her the rest of the way home.

* * *

"You're early," Dr. DiMarco said with a smile when Virginia entered the doctor's office, the bell above the door jangling to announce her arrival. He greeted her with a handshake, and her attention turned to how sweaty her palms were. The wrist inside her brace itched.

"To be early is to be on time," Virginia replied, wiping her palms on her slacks and clearing her throat before offering a nervous smile.

Dr. DiMarco chuckled and stepped around the large wooden desk, gesturing for Virginia to follow. On the desk, manila folders of papers were strewn about and a

"Is something the matter?" Dr. DiMarco wanted to know.

Virginia rustled through her bag to silence the device. Jack, this time. "No, I'm sorry. My kids," she explained.

"Do you need to go?" He pursed his lips and looked over his glasses at Virginia.

She shook her head, buried her phone back in her bag, and shoved the bag into one of the desk drawers.

"Please, continue."

Her phone rang three more times while Dr. DiMarco showed Virginia the ropes, but the ringtone was muffled enough contained within the purse and the drawer that the two both ignored it. Still, each time it rang, Virginia noticed Dr. DiMarco frown and felt her stomach sink.

The clock struck nine, and the first patients of the day filed in, one after the other. Dr. DiMarco greeted them warmly, and Virginia felt herself relax a bit as the doctor led the first patient back to an exam room.

"Excuse me," she called to a patient who sat reading a magazine across the room from Virginia. "What was your name?"

The patient gave her name, and Virginia found her file and pulled it, setting it aside for the doctor, and felt a tiny rush of pride. And then the phone rang.

The next two hours were a blur of phone calls and walk-ins, interrupted at irregular intervals by the persistent ringing of her cell phone as Marney and both of her children tried to reach her. Disoriented and unable to make out the small handwriting on most of the files, Virginia pulled the wrong patient files twice, and by the time the doctor came to talk with her during a break between patients, she was a flustered mess.

"Virginia." He opened his mouth and closed it again before exhaling and asking, "How do you feel like this is going?"

"I know I've made some mistakes, but I think once I get the hang of it..." She trailed off and looked up at him, tears coming to her eyes.

"It just seems like you've got a lot going on, like you're distracted."

"I am so sorry. I promise it's not usually like this." She shook her head vehemently.

Dr. DiMarco's eyes softened. "I understand, but with all the mistakes... Virginia, I think it might just be better for me to keep doing this myself for now."

The room seemed to spin and fall away from Virginia. She wrapped her fingers around the arms of her chair to steady herself.

"I've got an appointment with my eye doctor." The lie seemed to fall out of her mouth. "I've already scheduled it. They didn't have availability before my start date, but I've got an appointment next week." Dr. DiMarco considered what she was saying. "That should put an end to the mistakes with the files," she added when he didn't respond. "Please?"

At last, he sighed. "We'll give it two more weeks and see how it goes."

Virginia closed her eyes in relief and was surprised when she felt a tear roll down her cheek.

"Now, please go take care of whatever business is

causing such a distraction this morning. I'll take it from here."

She gathered her things and hurried from the room, offering a tentative smile on her way out the door before rooting in her purse for her phone. *Somebody better have died.*

CHAPTER 7

*V*irginia's cheeks burned as she pulled up in front of her house. Both her children's cars sat in her driveway, and Marney's was on the curb. Virginia pulled in behind Marney, cursing under her breath.

She crossed the neatly manicured lawn and turned the door handle. Inside, a silence fell—the kind that says, "We were just talking about you."

"What a surprise," Virginia said in a feeble attempt to sound affectionate.

"There you are!" Lucy emerged from the kitchen and wrapped her mother in an embrace in the entryway. "We brought food. Are you hungry?"

Virginia's stomach growled, but she doubted she could eat.

Before she could decline, Lucy's eyes went to the brace on Virginia's wrist and her expression turned concerned. "What happened to your wrist?"

"It's nothing," Virginia said. "It was feeling sore the

other day, and I'm just wearing this to appease Lawrence." She crossed the room without waiting for Lucy to question her lie.

In the small kitchen, Marney and Jack sat across from each other in the breakfast nook, dipping chips into bowls of salsa and melted cheese.

"The woman of the hour!" Marney said with a smile. "Where have you been? We were worried about you."

"I could tell." Virginia held up her phone. "Seventeen calls, between the three of you! In the span of two hours!"

Jack frowned. "Mom, you found a dead body yesterday. We were worried. We wanted to make sure you're okay. And what's with the brace?"

"I have a life, Jack," Virginia snapped, face flushing. "A life that was interrupted seventeen times this morning by your phone calls."

"Well, you could have answered one of them," Marney quipped.

"To answer your question, I'm fine." Virginia ignored Marney's remark. "My wrist is fine. I am fine. Everything is fine."

"Good." Marney smiled. "Now that I know you're not traumatized, I can be mad at you again for being an ass during my move-in."

"What happened?" Jack wanted to know.

Marney waved her hand in the air and said, "It's no big deal. Virginia is understandably upset with me for not telling her sooner that I was moving. She lashed out at one of the nurses."

"Mom!" Lucy's disapproval stung Virginia.

"Really, don't worry about it," Marney said, waving her

hand in the air again and shaking her head. "Virginia has certainly received more than enough karmic punishment for any wrongdoing."

Virginia's face burned again.

Lucy walked over to Virginia and wrapped her in a hug. "It's just so awful. And on Marney's very first day! Do they know what happened?"

Marney shrugged. "I think they're saying it was an accident."

"An accident?" Virginia's attention was piqued.

"Something to do with her blood thinners, I think. I heard someone saying she took too many and had a stroke."

"That's horrible!" Lucy cried.

"Are they looking into it any further?" Virginia asked.

"I'm not sure." Marney shrugged. "I know Breeze Village is hosting a small memorial for her on Tuesday." Marney gave Virginia a curious look, and Virginia shrugged, trying to dismiss the gnawing curiosity telling her something was wrong.

First, it was a natural death, so unremarkable police didn't even need to be called to the scene. Now it was an accident? Virginia had questions, and a memorial full of people who had known Ruth seemed like the place to get answers.

* * *

THE WEEKEND PASSED SLOWLY, interrupted by crippling anxiety every time Virginia remembered the bright yellow foreclosure notice and the potential salvation of a part-time secretarial job that at any moment could be revoked. On Monday she visited the eye doctor and had her prescription updated, and then on Tuesday morning she picked hydrangeas from her garden and arranged them in a vase to take to Marney's cottage. She was determined to go to the memorial service and learn more about Ruth, and she knew she owed Marney an apology.

The parking lot in front of Breeze Village was mostly empty. Tuesday mornings must not be prime visiting hours. Virginia had her pick of large parking spaces well away from other cars, and she carefully swung her little sedan into a spot in the far corner of the lot before making her way up the wooden stairs to the front door. The thin woman with the oxygen tank who had been knitting on the porch during Virginia's previous visit was there once again, and Virginia gave her a feeble wave with her free hand before pulling open the door and stepping into the cool lobby.

She greeted the receptionist. "I'm here to visit Marney Richards." She donned the visitor's badge and assured the receptionist she knew how to get to Marney's cottage before heading through the dining room and out into the courtyard.

This, it seemed, was where the memorial would be held. White folding chairs dotted the grass, all facing an easel which bore a large photograph of Ruth with a man Virginia assumed was her son Matt and a woman who must have been Matt's wife. The picture looked to have been taken here in Ruth's room at Breeze Village. Virginia made her way down the aisle between the folding chairs and wove around the blown-up photograph before proceeding to Marney's cottage. She took a deep breath before knocking on the door.

Though Virginia knew she owed Marney an apology for her reaction to Marney's move, she also felt she was due an apology for the commotion Marney's phone calls had caused on her first day of work, nearly costing her the job. Since she wasn't ready to tell Marney about the predicament she was facing with her home or her attempt to fix things by getting a job, she couldn't very well demand an apology. Instead, she exhaled and willed herself to let it go, never her strong suit.

When Marney swung the door back, she lit up in surprise and genuine delight to see her friend standing before her and wrapped Virginia in a hug. Though she had always been thinner than Virginia, and even more so in her old age, Marney gave strong, warm hugs. Virginia felt the tension inside her ease as she stood in her friend's embrace.

"I brought you these," she said, offering the vase of flowers to Marney.

"They're lovely." Marney took the vase and positioned it in the center of her small round dining table, moving aside the wicker napkin basket that previously occupied the space. "Thank you for bringing them, but I know you didn't come all the way here just to offer me flowers. What brings you here?"

"I owe you an apology."

Marney narrowed her eyes. "You want me to believe that you, Virginia Harold Walker, woman who can do no wrong, swallowed her pride and came here just to apologize to me?" She shook her head and clucked her tongue.

"You hate this place. Ever since Jack started on about how you should think about downsizing, you don't even like to drive past it."

Virginia shrugged and Marney let the topic go, pouring them each a glass of iced tea and leading Virginia into the living room. Though she'd been at Breeze Village less than a week, Marney had made the place feel like a home already. The familiar red-checkered loveseat and cushioned wicker rocking chair faced a small hutch with a TV perched on top. The walls were dotted with paintings Marney had collected from local artists over the years, alongside framed photos of Dylan growing up.

"I thought you were going to paint the place?"

"I still might, but I didn't want to put off making it feel like home until I get around to painting. Dylan is so busy at work lately, but I know I'll need her help to paint the place. I'm not sure when we'll be able to get to it."

On the television, a weatherman predicted a high near eighty and lots of sun. "Brilliant weather for the memorial," Marney said.

"Oh, is that today?" Virginia attempted a look of surprise.

"You walked past the chairs and everything to get here, didn't you?" Marney asked before her jaw dropped and she shook her head. "Wait a minute, that's *really* why you're here today, isn't it?"

"I told you, I came to offer my dearest and oldest friend a sincere, heartfelt apology for my indefensible behavior. But since I'm here, I think I'd like to go to the memorial. You know, since I found her and everything."

"Come off it." Marney shook her head. "I know this was your plan all along."

"I just feel like no one is asking questions or even giving her death a second thought. Just because she was ninety doesn't mean her death is irrelevant."

CHAPTER 8

Virginia and Marney were among the first to take their seats in the courtyard. Marney looked down at her wrist and then turned to Virginia with a shrug. "It's eleven. It should be starting now."

As the minutes ticked on, several more seats filled up. The knitting woman from the porch wheeled her oxygen tank behind her and chose a seat in the front. Virginia recognized Haley, the nurse, though instead of scrubs she was wearing a black dress. Virginia figured it must be her day off.

When a pantsuit-clad woman made her way to the front of the group, only half the chairs were occupied, and Virginia frowned. Ruth had lived at Breeze Village for years, and this was the turnout at her memorial?

"Thank you all for coming today," the woman began. She looked in her early fifties, gray-blond hair cut in a neat bob, and she wore thin-rimmed glasses and a black and white polka-dotted top under her charcoal suit. Virginia wondered if she always dressed so grimly or if she'd dressed for the occasion. "Most of you know me. I'm Michelle Martin, the owner of Breeze Village. In my role here, it is one of my greatest pleasures to get to know our residents. You all truly are the life of this home. And it is one of our greatest challenges to cope with loving and losing the residents who leave us."

As Michelle continued her speech, Virginia surveyed the crowd once again. Several nurses in scrubs wiped their eyes. One woman in the back made a show of crying loudly, but most of the attendees looked dazed or bored. A male nurse led a small, hunched woman to a seat in the back, his arm around hers while she pushed her rollator through the grass. Before she could sit down, she looked up and pointed at the photograph of Ruth and her family.

"There's that new nurse," she croaked. The nurse tried to quiet her, but she continued. "Mean little witch!"

Virginia looked from the woman to the photo and back.

"All right, Mrs. June, let's get you back to your room." The nurse began to guide her back toward the building, but Mrs. June shrugged him off with surprising force considering her small stature.

"Who are you?" Her voice was shrill and panicked. "Let go of me!"

"It's all right, Mrs. June. It's me, Anthony. I help take care of you. Let's get back to your room, okay?"

Anthony led the woman back inside, her fighting him the entire way, and when they were gone Michelle cleared her throat and resumed speaking, but Virginia didn't hear a word of the address. She felt nauseated, her ears ringing.

Marney looked over and grabbed Virginia's hand.

"I need a minute," Virginia whispered, then slipped from the courtyard into the dining room. Inside the French doors, catering staff carried in trays of food and set up for the luncheon to follow the memorial. Virginia turned down the hallway toward the bathroom to splash some water on her face, but when she passed Ruth's door, she saw it was open.

Inside, the room had been set up for residents to come and say their goodbyes. The bed was made, and a single rose sat atop the covers. A chair stood beside the bed so residents could sit with their memories of Ruth. Virginia wondered how many residents would make use of the opportunity. She walked around the room, brushing a finger over the top of the dark wooden dresser.

"What was your life like?" she whispered.

The sound of heavy footsteps in the hallway startled Virginia, and she ducked into Ruth's bathroom, pulling the door nearly shut and peering through the crack. A man she recognized as Ruth's son strode into the room, looked around, then stepped over to the bedside table, yanked out the small drawer, and rifled through it. Not finding whatever he was looking for, he shoved the drawer shut and moved on to the dresser to repeat the process. *What is he looking for?*

Virginia looked around her, hoping whatever he sought wasn't in the bathroom. To her right, a mirrored medicine cabinet on the wall hung ajar, and Virginia saw nearly a dozen pill bottles occupying the small shelves. The idea of an accident with dosing suddenly seemed plausible.

With one thin finger, she nudged the door open a little

more and saw that every one of the bottles had a colored cap with a timer on the top. On the back of the door, Ruth had taped a piece of paper with a handwritten medications schedule, neatly printed in blue ink. So maybe an accident wasn't so plausible after all.

She turned the bottles to face her and found the bottle of anticoagulants. *To be taken twice daily with water,* she read. The blue plastic timer cap displayed 146 hours. She found her pad of sticky notes in her purse and wrote the number 146 on it before returning it to her bag. Something about this didn't feel right.

As she turned back to the door to peer through the crack, the door swung open, and Virginia found herself face to face with Matt. He looked down at her, his brown eyes piercing.

"What are you doing here?" he demanded.

Virginia stuttered for a moment before blurting out, "I'm a friend of Ruth's."

"So you're rummaging through her bathroom?"

"I, uh…" Virginia stared up at Matt's scowling face, then puffed out her chest and collected herself. "I could ask you the same question. What are you doing here, rummaging through Ruth's drawers?"

"My mother's pocket watch wasn't returned to me with the rest of her personal effects. I was looking for it." Matt glowered down at her. "But it's clear suspicious people can come and go as they please. I'm sure it's long gone."

"The only suspicious things here are you and the idea that Ruth's death was an accident."

Virginia turned to see her oldest friend walking toward her and a veritable crowd forming in the dining room. Her senses seemed to come back to life, and suddenly she was aware of the aromas of Southern cooking and the bustle of a crowd ready to eat.

"Is the memorial service over?"

"Ended just a few minutes ago." Marney nodded. "And as a reward for sitting through the memorial for someone I didn't even know, I am going to indulge in some Miss B's."

"I knew it smelled like Miss B's!"

Marney started to turn and walk back to the dining room, but Virginia grabbed her arm and looked around to make sure no one was listening.

"I found something."

"What do you mean, you found something?"

"In Ruth's room." Marney frowned, and Virginia gave her a sheepish look. "I was just going to the bathroom to freshen up for a minute, but the door was open. They've got the room all set up for people to sit and process the loss, so it's not like it was off-limits or anything."

"So, what did you find?"

"Well, I was just in there processing her death, like people are *supposed* to be doing—I found her, so isn't it expected that I'd have some sort of trauma or complex feelings or something? Anyway, I was just there, and then out of nowhere there were footsteps, and I panicked and hid in the bathroom."

"A perfectly normal thing to do when you're somewhere you're totally allowed to be," Marney teased.

"I'm being serious. So I'm hiding in the bathroom,

peeking out the crack in the door, when in comes Ruth's son, Matt. I recognized him from the picture at the memorial. And he starts yanking open drawers like he's looking for something."

"What do you think he was looking for?"

"He said it was a pocket watch, but that's not the interesting part. While I was hiding, I saw inside Ruth's medicine cabinet. She had a ton of different prescriptions, so at first I thought it made sense that she might mess up a dose of something, but she had special caps on all the bottles with timers so she'd know when she last took each pill, and she had a schedule taped up on the inside of the cabinet. The woman was more organized than even Jack."

Marney gave Virginia a look of faux disbelief.

"The point is," Virginia continued, "it doesn't seem likely that she accidentally took too much of her medication."

"You said Matt told you he was looking for a pocket watch. You talked to him?"

Virginia nodded. "He wasn't happy to see me. He told me his mother 'deserves peace,' and that I was sticking my nose where it doesn't belong."

"He sounds pleasant."

"About as pleasant as poison ivy." Virginia opened her purse and rooted around inside. "I almost forgot. I looked at the timer cap on the blood thinners. How many days is 146 hours?"

Marney pulled out her phone and tapped away. "Six point oh eight three. So, about six days."

"And you moved in on Thursday? That was only five days ago."

Marney cocked her head to the side. "What are you thinking?"

"I'm thinking, how could Ruth have taken too many pills and dropped dead if she hadn't even taken that medication that day?"

"Maybe it doesn't act right away? Maybe she took too many the day before, but it didn't kill her until the next day. Or maybe whoever said it was the blood thinners was wrong, and we're looking at the wrong medication altogether." Marney shrugged, shook her head, and turned back to the dining room. "If you want to theorize about reasons a ninety-year-old woman might drop dead, can we at least do it over a plate of fried chicken?"

Virginia grabbed Marney's arm again. "Or someone else gave her the medications."

"The staff here seem really on top of everything, but I suppose it's possible."

"Or a son after an inheritance?"

Marney's eyes widened. Her voice almost a whisper, she asked, "Murder? There's no way."

"Can you just call Dylan? I want to tell the police about what I found, and about Matt acting suspicious."

Marney reluctantly agreed, and as she drifted to a corner of the lobby, phone to her ear, Virginia wandered into the dining room to see who from Breeze Village might know anything about Ruth's son Matt.

The dining room smelled heavenly, and it was all Virginia could do not to grab herself a plate of food while she waited for Marney to return, but she knew the wrath she'd face if Marney came back to find Virginia eating without her. Instead, she looked around at the lunching crowd. Whereas the memorial itself had been sparsely attended, it seemed like the whole of Breeze Village had come down for the food.

Across the room, she spied a table where a card game was just getting started. The best gossip always spread over a game of cards, and even if she didn't glean any useful information, she'd be keeping her hands busy while she waited for Marney to come back so she could eat.

She crossed the room and approached the table. Six of the eight chairs were taken, and she asked what game they were playing.

"Texas Hold 'Em," a portly man answered with a warm grin. He had a thick Southern accent and more enthusiasm than teeth.

"Mind if I join you?"

"Please do." He gestured to one of the two open seats and dealt out the cards.

"Did you all just come from the memorial? There seem to be more people here than there were outside."

"Ah, no, I never go to those," the man said, shaking his head. "I don't need nothing bringing me down at this age. But I always come to the luncheon. It ain't often we get Miss B's around here, and not all of us have family who come to take us out to lunch. I'm not saying the regular food's bad," he added, hands up, "but it ain't Miss B's."

Virginia nodded in understanding as the man turned over three cards in front of them all. The woman to Virginia's right moved two tokens into the center of the table.

"I was just surprised not to see more people at the memorial," Virginia said. "I thought Ruth had been here for years and knew everyone. I figured most of Breeze Village would come out to remember her."

"When you've been here a while, people dying sort of loses its sting," the woman said, her mouth turned down in a small frown as she looked from her cards to the ones in the center of the table and back. "I mean, don't get me wrong, I'm torn up over Ruth, if for no other reason than that I'll miss watching her kick Ronald's butt in these poker games."

"You're talking to the reigning Breeze Village Poker Champion," the man said to Virginia, pride apparent in his face.

"All I'm saying," the woman continued, "is that Ruth's death is a loss, and I think we'll all feel it, but that not all of us deal with it by turning up to sit in the gardens and listen to M&M give the same speech she gives every time."

"M&M?" Virginia asked.

"Michelle, the owner," the woman said. "Michelle Martin. She's nice and all, but when you've heard her give one speech, you've heard them all."

Ronald flipped over another card and the woman folded, tossing her cards face-down in front of her before reaching into her bag and pulling out a tube of lipstick and a small mirror.

"Someone told me Ruth messed up the dose of one of her medications and that's why she died." Virginia looked around the table to gauge the reactions of her competitors, but if they found the statement alarming, they all had amazing poker faces. "Does that sound like Ruth?"

"I'd wager almost everyone here has missed a pill or taken two of something," said a small man in a wheelchair who had so far been silent. "But not Ruth. Ruth was the most meticulously organized woman I've ever met."

The rest of the table nodded in agreement.

"I guess you just never really know someone," the woman next to Virginia said as she dabbed at her freshly-applied lipstick. The fuschia color made her teeth look yellowed.

Ronald turned over the last card, and the table erupted in groans. Ronald put his cards on the table face up. "Full house," he said with his toothless grin.

The man in the wheelchair started to congratulate Ronald when Virginia placed her cards on the table.

"Four eights," she said with a sly smile. "It was a pleasure playing with you."

She stood and shook Ronald's hand just as Marney approached the table.

"There you are!" she said. "Dylan said she's busy, but she's sending—"

"It was great to meet you all," Virginia said abruptly, cutting Marney off. She waved to the table of poker players as Ronald began to deal out another round and led Marney away. She looked around before giving Marney a nod that it was okay to continue talking, and Marney rolled her eyes at the secrecy.

"As I was trying to tell you, Dylan can't come right now, but she's sending another officer to take your statement."

Virginia frowned. "Why can't Dylan make it?"

"She didn't say, but she's been really busy lately. Some kind of gang bust, I'm not sure. But she promised someone would be over soon to talk with you."

Virginia nodded and poured herself a cup of red fruit punch. "I'm going to go wait for him in the lobby."

Suddenly, her appetite had disappeared. She wanted to feel excited and hopeful: she had information that might convince someone to look into Ruth's death, to get answers for this woman who deserved them. But instead, she felt dread building in the pit of her stomach as she took a seat by the window and waited for the officer to arrive.

* * *

WHEN THE SQUAD car pulled up outside, Virginia rose quickly and stepped out the door to greet him on the porch. The rocking chairs were all empty; everyone was inside enjoying their lunch.

"Hi, I'm Virginia," she said, extending her hand.

The officer took it and gave it a limp shake. "Officer Matthews. What seems to be the problem?"

Virginia stepped back and looked around. "Oh, my mistake, you must be here for someone else. I don't have a problem. I just have some information on a case."

"Which case is that?"

"It's about the recent death of one of the residents here. Ruth... I don't know her last name."

The officer looked down at a clipboard he held in his hand. "There's no open investigation into the death of any Breeze Village residents." The man was so short he had to look up to meet Virginia's eyes, and a thick mustache hung down over his disinterested frown.

"Well, I think my information might prompt you to investigate."

"What is it, then?" the officer asked impatiently.

Virginia looked around again. "Are you sure Dylan Richards couldn't come? I've known her forever, and I'd really feel more comfortable talking with her."

"She's on another investigation. Now, what did you want to share?"

Virginia took a deep breath. "Well, they've got Ruth's room set up for residents to come and visit with her, to process their grief, and I was in there during the memorial today, and I saw her son." She waited for the officer to give a reaction, but he didn't. "He was acting suspicious, rifling through her drawers."

"Did you talk to him? Did he say what he was doing?"

"He told me he was looking for a pocket watch, but he got incredibly defensive when I suggested Ruth's death might not be an accident. Told me to stop poking my nose where it doesn't belong, like he didn't want anyone looking into it."

"Why'd you tell him you think it wasn't an accident?"

"People are saying Ruth had a stroke because she took too many of one of her prescriptions, the blood thinners, but she had timer caps on all her pill bottles and was more organized with her pills than anyone I've ever seen. An accidental overdose just seems so unlikely."

"You know, sometimes people get old and decide they're ready to go."

Virginia opened her mouth in shock at the officer's suggestion. "Ruth had plenty to live for," she said more aggressively than she intended. "She was social and well-loved. And besides, I wasn't finished telling you: she hadn't even taken the medication in question on the day she died. The timer cap said the last time it was opened was the day before."

The officer made a few notes on his clipboard, nodded to Virginia, and turned back to his car. "Thank you for your information, ma'am. If we have any further questions, we'll be in touch."

"So, are you going to investigate?"

Officer Matthews walked around to the driver's side of the squad car and opened the door before looking back up at Virginia. "I can't comment on that. I appreciate your concern, and like I said, we'll be in touch if we need anything else from you."

He climbed into the car and drove off, leaving Virginia alone on the porch.

When Virginia reentered the dining room, she found Marney sitting at a table by herself, happily gnawing at a fried chicken drumstick. A full plate of chicken and macaroni and cheese sat next to Marney's own nearly empty plate.

"I got you some," Marney said between bites. "But I didn't wait for you to dig in."

Virginia smiled feebly. "Thanks." She picked up one piece of chicken and took a small bite.

"Uh oh, the conversation with the officer didn't go well?" When Virginia gave Marney a questioning look, Marney added, "I've never seen you less excited to eat Miss B's chicken, or anything, for that matter. You're clearly upset."

"I don't know." Virginia shrugged. "He was just so dismissive. I wish Dylan had been able to come out here. I asked him if they were going to look into it, and he just said he'd contact me if they have questions."

"Want to come back to the cottage and watch bad daytime TV to take the edge off?" Marney suggested.

Virginia shook her head. "I'm a little tired. I think I'll just head home."

"Suit yourself. But next time you visit me, don't lie about why you're here. And come to see me, not just to snoop around at a stranger's funeral, you hear?"

Virginia put on her best smile before she stood and made her way back to her car across the parking lot. She wouldn't be back. How could she ever set foot in that building without thinking of a dead woman sitting in a leather recliner and how no one cared how she ended up that way? No, Virginia didn't think she could stand to come back, but she couldn't tell Marney that. At least not yet.

CHAPTER 10

On Thursday morning, Virginia donned a pair of white linen capris and a green floral top and spritzed herself with perfume. She wiggled her wrist back and forth, finally able to leave the brace off. Excitement bubbled up inside her, and a genuine smile came to her lips as she brushed rouge onto her cheeks in front of the mirror. She'd missed the last bi-weekly neighborhood tea party and only heard later that Jan had brought her controversial pineapple cheese casserole and Dorothea had shared pictures of her new, much-younger boyfriend. She hoped this week's gathering would be as eventful.

Virginia was essentially born into the Grove Park social scene, and she enjoyed feeling at the center of it all. Her own mother had begun hosting the regular tea parties with the other neighborhood women when Virginia was in primary school, and she'd sat on the stairs and peered through the railing when they gathered, watching the women sip spiked punch and gossip. She hadn't started attending the gatherings until her mother had gotten sick. Virginia would bring her in her wheelchair and attend to her, soaking up the background of gossip and strong friendships. As hard as it was, caring for her mother at the end of her life, those social gatherings were a bright spot, and the women of Grove Park welcomed her into the fold with open arms.

The tea parties' average age had become closer to Virginia's own age in the years following. The original attendees made way for their daughters to take their places, and Virginia was the group's de facto leader. For years she called around, made sure enough people were bringing food and that two people wouldn't inadvertently bring the same dish, and coordinated the location so they all took turns hosting. Lately, though, Kim had stepped up and started taking over. After Virginia forgot the January gathering altogether, Kim had taken the lead, and Virginia graciously smiled, thanked her, and pretended not to be hurt.

This week's tea party was at Kim's house, and as Virginia stood in the doorway, a tray of butter cookies in hand, she tamped down her anxiety and smiled. It was good to feel normal again, to put aside the thoughts of Ruth and Officer Matthews that had been plaguing her.

"Come in!" Kim said with enthusiasm as she swung the door open. Her eyes went to the dish in Virginia's hands and lit up. "Please tell me those are your mother's butter cookies!" She took the tray from Virginia, letting out an anticipatory moan of delight, and gestured through the impeccable foyer to an equally clean and put-together living room. "We're all in the living room. Make yourself at home while I pop this in the kitchen."

Virginia looked around the entryway where she stood. Dark hardwood floors gleamed, and photographs of Kim's children and grandchildren neatly adorned the bright white walls. Not a single surface bore a speck of dust, nor a sticky note reminder. Through the arched doorway, the living room was lively with conversation. The floral upholstered couch held three women who were gesticulating wildly while arguing about whether the vendors at the farmers' market actually grew the vegetables locally. Eleanor swore she'd seen Bob Warner at the supermarket buying peppers and then reselling them at the farmers' market for double the price the weekend before.

"Virginia!" A large black woman in a bright pink dress stood and embraced her. "We missed you last time."

"Not as much as I missed you, Gemma. You're looking radiant as ever."

"It's all the yoga," Gemma said. "I go downtown to the park for an hour every morning and watch those lovely ladies." She threw her head back and let out a deep belly laugh.

Virginia greeted the rest of the guests before sitting in one of the ornate wooden dining chairs Kim had brought into the room to seat the visitors. When they had all filled their cups with rum punch and plates with sandwiches and treats, Dorothea turned to Virginia and asked about Marney's move to Breeze Village.

"I know she wasn't ever the most social with us Grove Park ladies, but I was surprised to hear she moved to

thinners by accident. She was on a dozen different medications—aren't we all?—so an accident makes sense."

The ladies nodded and turned their attention back to the sandwiches on their plates, and a few began to resume their other conversations.

As the attention drifted from her to other topics, Virginia cleared her throat. "I don't think it was an accident, though."

At this, eyebrows raised and the attention was back on Virginia.

"What makes you say that?" Jan wanted to know, eyes narrowed.

"I saw the inside of her medicine cabinet. Ruth—that's her name—was meticulously organized. She had a handwritten schedule of her medications and timer caps on all the bottles, so she knew when she last took them. I can't see her making a mistake."

"You think it was a suicide? Like, she took all those pills on purpose?" Dorothea asked.

"Or a murder? I saw on TV where a man forced this woman to take an entire bottle of pills at gunpoint," Jan added.

Virginia shrugged, unable to keep from basking a little in the undivided attention she was being shown. "The weird thing is, the pills in question hadn't even been opened since the day before she died. I did see her son rooting through her drawers, and when I suggested there was something suspicious about Ruth's death, he practically jumped down my throat."

"Do you think he had something to do with it?" Even Kim was wrapped up in the story now.

"I don't know." Virginia shrugged again and frowned. "I tried to talk to the police, but the officer didn't even seem to be listening to me. I don't think they're going to investigate."

"Well, you should solve it," Dorothea said as if it was the most obvious conclusion in the world. "Then you'll get the reward money."

"You old fool," Jan said, swatting her arm at Dorothea. "There is no reward money."

"Well, a woman from my water aerobics class said she was walking to her car from the Piggly Wiggly, the one over on Beaufort Avenue, and she saw a man with a gun holding up another guy. She said she called and gave a description of the guy and what she saw, and she got $1000 when they caught the guy because of her report. Crime Stoppers, I think it was, that gave her the money."

"That woman is lying to you," Jan insisted. "For attention."

"No, it's true," Gemma said, nodding. "Her daughter is one of my yoga girls. She always wears the cutest little tops. Anyway, I heard her talking to her friends about it too."

The debate continued for most of the gathering, and Virginia said nothing. If it were true that Dorothea's friend had earned a $1,000 reward for helping to solve a robbery case, she wondered what the reward would be like for solving a murder.

THE NEXT MORNING as Virginia lay in bed, fighting the recurring battle between wanting to sleep and needing to pee, a knock at the door caught her attention. She lay still, thinking that if it were Lawrence he'd let himself in. When no key turned in the lock, she rolled herself out of bed with considerable effort, used the toilet, and donned her robe. She hoped whoever was at the door had given up by the time she answered it.

They hadn't.

Instead, a woman who looked in her early forties stood before her wearing a pink pantsuit, leopard print heels, and bright pink lipstick to match her suit. Gold dangled from her ears, neck, and wrists, and gleamed on at least five of her fingers.

"Can I help you?" Virginia asked the woman, whose smile felt more intimidating than assuring.

"Good morning." The woman's voice was sickly sweet. "My name is Chelsea, and I'm here on behalf of Bellemeade Property Developers." When Virginia gave only a puzzled look in response, the woman continued, "I'm here because we want to buy your house."

Virginia continued to stare at the woman in confusion. "I'm sorry, I think there's been a mistake. My house isn't for sale."

The woman laughed, and Virginia wondered what she'd said that was funny. "Don't you worry," the woman said, her voice condescending, as if she were talking to a child. "Virginia, right?" Virginia nodded, her confusion now edged with concern as the woman knew her name. "I know it's not up on the market, but Bellemeade has big plans for this area, and we can make you a strong offer."

"I'm really not looking to sell right now," Virginia said again, backing into her entryway and starting to close the door.

"Don't you want to know our offer?" Chelsea asked, catching the door before Virginia could close it, her smile unfaltering.

Virginia felt like a trapped animal. She felt herself give a small nod, and Chelsea's smile grew, not touching her eyes. She handed Virginia a piece of paper and pointed to a figure at the bottom. $100,000? That didn't seem right.

"I'm pretty sure this house is worth more."

"Oh, don't you worry," Chelsea said again. "It's probably been a while since you looked into the property value, right? Bellemeade always gives a fair offer, and we'll make everything so easy for you."

Virginia shook her head and tried to hand back the paper. Chelsea didn't take it from her. "Look, I'm really not interested, but thank you for your offer."

"If you'd like to take this as a starting point and negotiate from there, we're always happy to work with you."

Virginia shook her head again and insisted that she wasn't interested in selling, no matter the price. This was her home, and she intended for her children to inherit it when she was gone.

Chelsea's sickly sweet smile dropped. "You're going to be a fighter, aren't you?"

Virginia stood a little straighter and smiled. "Yes, I am."

Before Chelsea could get another word in, Virginia closed the door on her and turned the lock. *I am a fighter.* As she turned on her coffee pot, she felt awake even as it began to brew. She was a fighter. She'd always been a fighter. When the university had tried to suspend Earl for talking about evolution in one of his lectures. When her mother had been sick and the doctors tried to pass it off as nothing. Virginia had always been a fighter, but she'd forgotten that lately. Not anymore. Ruth deserved to have someone fighting to know what happened to her, and Virginia was going to be that person.

CHAPTER 11

That evening, without thinking about it, Virginia found herself in her car heading toward Breeze Village. Her newfound sense of purpose and exhilaration faded as the main building came into sight. The last time she was here, she'd sworn she wouldn't be back, and now her throat burned as she remembered the hopelessness she'd felt when Officer Matthews had dismissed her.

"What are you doing here?" she whispered to herself as she pulled into the parking lot, turning the car off but making no move to get out. She took deep breaths in and out, trying to reconnect with her fighting spirit.

Knock, knock.

A rap at her window made Virginia jump, and she turned to see Marney standing beside her car. She rolled down her window.

"What are you doing?" Marney asked.

"I'm not sure," Virginia said honestly. She wasn't sure

what she was looking for at Breeze Village, but she knew it was where she needed to start if she were to find answers about Ruth's death. Matt had been looking for something in Ruth's room. Maybe someone here had ideas about what it was or whether anyone but her son had something to gain from Ruth's death.

"Just seemed like a nice day to sit in your car in the parking lot?" Marney teased.

Virginia forced a laugh and climbed out of the car. "What else is there to do on a Friday night when you're eighty?"

"Eat pizza and watch bad TV?" Their old Friday night ritual.

Virginia nodded and followed Marney to her cottage.

When Virginia first met Marney, she didn't know what Marney was running from, but she knew it was bad. After Virginia spotted them sleeping in their car near the elementary school, Marney and Dylan lived with Virginia and Earl and the kids for two months before they were able to get their own tiny, rundown apartment. Long after they moved out, every Friday, Virginia's doorbell would ring, and she'd answer the door to find Marney and Dylan on the porch, holding hands, Marney looking so scared she was about to cry. "Pizza night?" she'd ask, and Virginia would agree and bring them inside and turn on the TV.

It was only later that Marney told Virginia about Dean, about the life she'd left behind, about the memories that haunted her and caused her panic attacks. Fridays had been the worst of Dean's drinking days. He'd go out with the guys, gamble, and drink. On his winning days, he'd come home so happy, promising Marney a new life, a bigger house, a car that turned on every time you turned the key in the ignition. But on the losing days, he'd come home mad, and nothing was safe from his anger.

Earl had never once suggested to Virginia that Marney and Dylan should spend less time at their house. Virginia had never told him what Marney shared with her about her life before Seaview. He'd never asked. Until the cancer spread, he'd go mow Marney's lawn every time he did his own. Marney and Dylan were invited to every holiday meal. Earl swung by with groceries when he knew they were having a hard time. Virginia loved him for it.

"Has Dylan said anything more about Ruth's death?" Virginia asked Marney between bites of pizza while Marney flipped through the channels on her television. She shook her head.

"Nope. Why?"

"I just wondered if they were looking into it any further after the info I gave them on Matt and the timer caps on the pills."

"I can try to ask her," Marney said. "But I know she's deep in whatever case she's working on, so I don't even know how much she knows about this."

"That's all right," Virginia said, shaking her head.

Marney settled on *House Hunters* and turned up the volume, setting the remote aside. The two of them tried to guess which house each couple would pick, but Virginia's heart wasn't in it. Every time the prices of the homes flashed on the screen, she just saw the yellow notice reminding her that her home might not be hers any longer. But she had a job, she reminded herself. It was only a matter of a few months before she'd be able to pay the lien, and, in the meantime, she'd get on a payment plan. Or, she couldn't stop herself from thinking, she could prove to the police that Ruth's death wasn't an accident. She could fight for justice for someone who deserved it and save her house with the reward money. If there was any reward money to be had, that is.

"Another?" Marney asked when the episode ended, but Virginia shook her head. "What's with you? You picked the wrong house for every couple, and this wasn't even a hard episode. Every single one of them went with the obvious pick."

"I think maybe the pizza just isn't sitting right with me," Virginia lied. "I'm going to head out."

The lobby was empty, and Virginia's footsteps echoed as she walked through on her way to the parking lot. In the dimly lit space, Virginia noticed the small office jutting off the lobby and, without thinking, crossed the open space and turned the door handle. To her surprise, it was unlocked. She slipped inside and shut the door behind her.

Inside, filing cabinets and bookshelves bursting with binders lined the office walls. On a thick wooden desk sat a sleek, modern monitor and keyboard, out of place among the dusty shelves and worn office chair. To her left was a door to the nurses' station, where residents' prescriptions were stored, and to her right was a small bathroom. Virginia turned her attention to the computer. She jiggled the mouse, but the monitor screen stayed dark. Frowning, she turned to the cabinets behind her and pulled out one of the drawers of files. *If I can just find Ruth's file, maybe it'll have Matt's address.*

Visions of staking out Matt's house came to her head. She could picture herself ducked down in the driver's seat of her car, spying across the street, calling Dylan to rush in with squad cars the moment Matt did something to give himself up. In this daydream, Dylan personally handed Virginia the reward money and Virginia personally told Chelsea, the property developer, to go screw herself.

If she could only remember Ruth's last name... Virginia knew it was something old-fashioned. Beauregard? Wilmont? She flipped through the files as quickly as she could.

The creak of the office door opening startled her, and Virginia turned to find a small woman with a disproportionately large nose and a walking cane standing in the doorway.

"I'm sorry," Virginia said instinctively, straightening up from where she'd been hunched over the open drawer of file folders.

"Sorry for what?" the woman asked. Virginia thought there was a hint of a smile on the woman's lips. She wore all black, slacks and a ruffled blouse, and her cane was slick black with a pearlescent white grip at the top.

"I, um, I got turned around," Virginia said, not answering the question.

"I see." The woman nodded. Though she was small, she exuded power. Virginia continued to stand still, and the woman continued to stare back at her. "Do you need help to get un-turned around?"

At that, Virginia's legs resumed functioning, and she hurried out of the office without another word. She turned to look back once when she'd halfway crossed the lobby and saw the woman still standing in the doorway, watching Virginia leave. She smiled and gave Virginia a wave, and Virginia turned back around and made her way to her car as quickly as she could.

CHAPTER 12

Virginia worked at the doctor's office Saturday. With her new prescription, she no longer struggled to make out the names on the patient files, but with every file she pulled, she remembered the jolt of fear she'd felt in the Breeze Village office the night before, hunting for Ruth's file and then being caught red-handed. Dr. DiMarco hadn't commented on her performance or said she could stay on indefinitely, but he hadn't threatened to fire her again, so she was feeling more at ease and looking forward to her first paycheck soon. Saturdays were busy days, as everyone who worked a regular 9-5 tried to schedule their appointments during Dr. DiMarco's limited weekend hours. Virginia's mind was occupied by the tasks at hand for most of the day, though she jumped with a start every time the door opened and caught her by surprise.

She'd been so close to finding another piece of information on Ruth. Her gut told her that if she could find Matt, she could find answers. Instead, there was a mysterious resident who had caught her sneaking around, and now Virginia wasn't sure what her next move should be.

When Sunday morning rolled around, Virginia still didn't know what her next move should be, but she figured Breeze Village was the place to try to figure it out. She swung by Marney's favorite bakery to pick up donuts before heading to Breeze Village and knocking on Marney's door.

This time, instead of an embrace, Marney greeted Virginia with a look of suspicion. "To what do I owe the pleasure?"

"Do I need a reason to bring my best friend donuts?"

"Truth: are you here because you enjoy spending time with me here in my new home, or because you want to ask me again whether Dylan has said anything about Ruth's death, and then when I say no, you're going to ask me to reach out to her about it?"

"Truth: neither," Virginia said. Marney raised an eyebrow at Virginia's response, and Virginia sighed. "Almost the second thing, but not quite. I am still very much hung up on Ruth's death, but I have accepted that the police are not doing their jobs—this is not about Dylan, just the rest of them—so I'm going to have to do it for them."

Marney frowned. "I'm not sure I follow. Play detective?"

"Ask around." Virginia shrugged and tried to sound nonchalant. "Just talk to the people who knew her best, who might have known her son. See what they have to say."

"I don't know." Marney took a donut from the box and bit into it, unconvinced by Virginia's plea.

"Listen, there's more." Virginia set down her own donut and leaned in closer. "Friday night, on my way out, I snuck into the office off the lobby."

"You what?"

Virginia recounted the story of going into the office and flipping through the file folders in search of Ruth's file. "If I could have remembered her last name, I'd have found it in time."

"It's Beaumont."

"Beaumont! That's it!" Virginia cursed under her breath. "Anyway, I was too slow, and then I was interrupted."

"By who?"

"I wish I knew." Virginia described the woman, and Marney frowned.

"Could be Genie," she offered.

"You know her?"

"Not well. She's in a bunch of the clubs, including the gardening club. I've seen her around."

"Well, I want to know what she was doing in that office."

"Because no one would possibly sneak into the office unless they had nefarious motives, right?" Marney gave Virginia a pointed look. "Anyway, I met someone at dinner last night. Her name is Colleen, and she's a psychic. If you're hellbent on asking around about Ruth, maybe you should talk to her. Maybe she can channel Ruth's spirit or something."

Virginia didn't believe in psychics, but she did believe

veritably haunted ever since by questions of what happened to the poor woman."

"I see. And you want me to commune with her spirit to seek answers?"

"Can you do that?" Virginia asked eagerly.

"I cannot." Colleen's curt response quashed Virginia's hope as soon as it arose. "I said I have connections with the spirit world, but it is more that they have a connection to the earthly world through me. I cannot ask of them, only receive guidance as it is given."

Virginia turned to Marney, expecting them to stand and take their leave, but instead, Marney smiled and said, "That is so fascinating! What kinds of readings do you offer for those of us on the earthly plane?"

Colleen looked the two of them up and down. "I do not offer." She said the word "offer" as if it were a dirty word. "I look into your soul, and I give you what you need. Today, you need to look inside yourself," she said, directing her gaze at Virginia.

"I think I'm good, actually," Virginia said. She made to stand but couldn't quite lift herself from the soft, sunken couch cushion.

"Oh, come on," Marney said. "It'll be fun."

Colleen redirected her attention back to Marney with a frown. "What I do is not for entertainment. It is for enlightenment." She turned back to Virginia. "Your hand, please."

Virginia glanced at Marney, who wore the expression of a child chided by their schoolteacher, then hesitantly extended her arm, placing her hand in Colleen's own outstretched palm. Colleen held Virginia's hand, palm facing up, and traced the soft skin in circles with her fingers before lowering her thick, round-rimmed glasses from the top of her head and bringing her face close to Virginia's palm.

"Strong lines," she said in a low voice. "Your heart line is curved, relatively short. You keep your emotions close to your chest." Colleen said it as a statement, not a question, and didn't look up to Virginia to confirm. Instead, she moved along. "There's a break in the line. You lost a love too soon. I'm so sorry."

Virginia almost pulled her hand back. She felt Marney's soft touch on her knee and remembered Marney holding her up at Earl's funeral, getting Jack and Lucy ready for school for weeks afterward. She cleared her throat to try to dislodge the lump that was forming. She'd come here to find out about Ruth, not to revisit her own suffering.

Before Virginia could end the reading, Colleen straightened up and looked around. "How does your ankle feel?" she asked, and Virginia replied that it was fine. Colleen frowned. "That's interesting. I'm suddenly overcome by the aroma of apples and cinnamon." She shrugged and offered up a smile. "Interference from the spirit world. They must be having a late breakfast."

With a chuckle, she returned her attention to Virginia's hand. "This is your life line. You've taken good care of yourself, although it's a bit weak here toward the end. Not surprising, at our age. But here!" Colleen gasped and yanked Virginia's arm, tugging her hand closer. "A fate line! Not everyone possesses one. What a treat."

Virginia and Marney exchanged looks as Colleen ran a

polished finger back and forth on Virginia's palm. If she didn't feel so scrutinized, the sensation might have been pleasant, but the gentle tickle felt ominous accompanied by Colleen's dissecting gaze.

"A change is coming for you," Colleen said with a nod. "Are you moving? I sense a change in location, leaving somewhere you have strong roots."

At this, Virginia yanked her hand back and tried to stand, growing flustered when she couldn't lift herself from the sofa. "I am not," she said. "And I have to go."

Marney stood and offered Virginia a hand, thanking Colleen for her time while Virginia left the room without so much as a goodbye. She'd nearly reached the elevators at the end of the hallway when Marney caught up with her.

"That wasn't quite what I expected," Marney said.

"What a quack."

"Some of it was interesting."

"'You lost a love, didn't you?' I'm eighty years old, of course I've lost a love. Everyone has, by this age."

Marney shrugged. The elevator chimed and the doors opened on the main level. As the two crossed the lobby, a tall man with icy white hair smiled at them and gave a small wave, which Marney returned.

"Who's that?" Virginia wanted to know, but Marney was too busy watching the man walk down the hallway and out of sight to notice Virginia's question.

* * *

THE NEXT MORNING when Virginia rose from the bed, she unconsciously found herself flexing her ankles, wiggling her feet before she planted them on the ground and lifted herself out of bed. She shook her head at herself. *You're being crazy.* Colleen hadn't said one single thing that rang true for Virginia that wouldn't have been true for everyone else her age. Except for that bit about an impending move.

After turning on her coffee pot, she meandered from the kitchen into the dining room and rifled through the papers on the long buffet table until she found once again the yellow notice reminding her she could lose her house if she didn't come up with nearly ten grand, and fast. She knew she needed to call the number on the notice, ask about deadlines and payment plans, take even the tiniest concrete step toward dodging this freight train heading straight for her. But at the thought of picking up the phone, she felt so overwhelmed she could hardly move, even just to tuck the notice back under the pile of unopened mail.

At work, Virginia devoted herself to impressing Dr. DiMarco. Even if she could bring herself to pick up the phone and inquire about payment plans to save her house, she needed to earn the money in the first place, and with her vision improved and a few shifts under her belt, she was beginning to feel like she could actually make this work. She felt herself sit up a little straighter, shoulders back and chin up, with a sense of purpose driving her movements.

"Mrs. Swain, for her annual," Virginia said, handing Dr. DiMarco a manila folder of papers. Then, in a lowered voice, she said, "Her daughter just turned forty-five and got a puppy for her grandson."

Dr. DiMarco gave her a gleaming smile before calling Mrs. Swain's name and escorting the woman back to an exam room. Virginia could hear him inquiring about her daughter and grandson as they walked, and she smiled.

Though her work wasn't anything exceptionally difficult, she felt energized by bringing a bit of herself to the job. Everyone loved to feel special, to feel like the people in their lives remembered them and thought of them in the intervals between meetings. With her love for gossip and genuine interest in the lives of others, Virginia had a knack for giving people that feeling. She glanced down at the post-it beside her hand. *Daughter age 45, puppy for grandson.* "My system works just fine," she whispered to herself before taking another sip of coffee and turning back to the schedule in front of her.

During a lull between patients, Virginia pulled up the Seaview Gazette's online edition and read from the headlines:

Wells County School Officials Plan to Appeal Judge's Order to Reinstate Teacher

Town Hall Features New Art Exhibit Showcasing Child Artists

Elm Creek Assemblage Construction Begins: Neighboring Communities' Opinions Divided

Police Chief Todd Rumored to be Stepping Down

Virginia's eyebrows raised in curiosity. *I wonder if Dylan knows about that.* She clicked the link and jotted a reminder on her pad of sticky notes to ask Marney about it.

As she scrolled through the article, she saw a link to the website of the Wells County police and clicked it. The front page bore an image of a line of officers in crisp uniforms on police motorcycles. Below, there was an assortment of links: citizen feedback, report a crime, become a deputy, records services, crime maps and statistics, and report a traffic complaint. Virginia clicked through the pages. She considered filling out a complaint form for the way Officer Matthews had dismissed her or reporting Ruth's death as a crime to make sure an investigation was opened. She scrolled further. At the bottom of the page was another link: get involved.

Click.

At the top of this page was the link to a ride-along application, and underneath were photographs of officers smiling, posing with the children of the community, with links to information on volunteer programs and internships. She clicked the link to the ride-along application and considered it. It would give her a way to get into the police station, perhaps give her a chance to poke around and find out whether there had been any investigation into Ruth's death. With any luck, the officer she'd ride along with wouldn't be Officer Matthews, and maybe they would be more interested in hearing what she had to say about Ruth's death.

Before she could do anything else, the bell over the door jangled and a young mother with twin toddlers herded them into the waiting room and approached the desk. Virginia quickly returned to her scheduling program. While the woman filled out the intake form, the boys played dinosaurs with each other, and Virginia wrote on a sticky note, *love dinosaurs, both want to be a T-Rex.* She'd tell Dr. DiMarco, and the boys' faces would light up when he casually mentioned the T-Rex during their check-ups, she knew.

As the day picked up, Virginia didn't have another opportunity to revisit the police website, but the station was on her way home. Instead of driving past, Virginia pulled into the parking lot in front of the station and watched the squad cars pulling in and out. She wondered whether any of them would drive past Matt's house, whether he was on the police's radar at all.

The waves lapped at Virginia's soft skin, and she felt her hair swirl around her. She exhaled slowly to stop her teeth from chattering. Despite the cold, the ocean water calmed Virginia, and she held her breath and ducked under the waves, feeling small as she bobbed in the churning sea.

It was barely dawn, the seagulls just beginning to cry out when Virginia finally dragged herself from the water and toweled off. She'd brought a bag of stale pretzels and fished it from her tote, tossing the snacks to the eager recipients.

Sitting on her towel, clothed in mostly dry sweatpants and wrapped in a shawl, Virginia watched the sun rise over the horizon. She had concocted a plan the night before— a plan that, if she could gather the courage, would be in motion a mere hour from now. Before going to work, she would stop at the police station and walk to the payphone down the street. She would call in a welfare check on Matt, say she's a friend of his but hasn't heard from him in days, that he was supposed to meet her the night before but never showed up. The police would send someone to Matt's address to check on him, and she would follow them there to see where he lived, then stake the place out later that evening.

Is it a crime to call in a welfare check on someone you don't actually have any reason to believe is in trouble? She wouldn't be reporting a fake crime, but she would be diverting police resources.

And if Marney ever found out…

Marney was more protective of Dylan than Virginia suspected most grizzly bears were of their cubs. It wasn't until Dean had turned his anger on Dylan that Marney considered leaving. She could take his abuse in order to provide for Dylan and protect her, but when he struck Dylan, it was all over. They were gone that very night, with no place to go. Marney had always done whatever it took to make sure Dylan was well-cared-for, and even now that Dylan was grown, a police captain vying for Assistant Chief, if Marney found out Virginia had done anything that risked drawing condemnation on Dylan at work, she would be furious.

As Virginia gathered her things to walk back to her car, her stomach turning flips with excitement and anxiety over the impending plan, a familiar voice called her name. She looked up to find Marney walking down the sandy path through the trees right toward her.

"I hoped I'd find you here," she said with a wave.

"What are you doing here?" Virginia tried to sound casual, not accusatory, but from Marney's facial expression, she guessed she missed the mark.

"I have news." A smile came to Marney's lips and crinkles formed around her eyes. "I went on a date."

"A date! It's about time!" Marney had only been on a handful of dates in the decades Virginia knew her. When they got the news that Dean had passed, Virginia hoped Marney would finally feel comfortable opening herself up again, but Marney had remained as contentedly solitary as ever. "What kind of man could catch the eye of the ever-unavailable Marney Richards?"

"A tall, handsome former attorney, that's who," Marney said. "Actually, I think you saw him the other day. When we were in the lobby after your reading with Colleen, a man walked by and smiled at us. Do you remember him?"

"I thought I sensed something between the two of you! Tell me everything," Virginia commanded, spreading her towel back out in the sand and offering Marney the remainder of the stale pretzels she'd been feeding to the birds.

Marney recounted with bubbling enthusiasm the dinner she'd shared with Byron the night before. He'd seen her coming out of a crochet class and then tried talking with her over meals a few times before finally asking her out to dinner. He'd taken her to a steakhouse downtown, paid for the meal, and asked her permission before kissing her goodnight. Marney was smitten.

"After he retired, he continued to take on pro bono work until recently, working for free in his retirement. I'm telling you, Virginia, he's special."

Marney continued to gush until the sun had fully risen and Virginia needed to get home to clean up before going to work. She'd lost the extra time she'd allotted for her plan at the police station, so it would have to wait until after work, but it was worth it to see her friend glowing like this.

"There's one more thing," Marney said as they were getting into their cars. "I didn't want to tell you this, but I can't keep it from you. But promise me you'll keep your cool."

"You didn't get married at the courthouse on your first date, did you?" Virginia joked.

Marney didn't crack a smile. Instead, she took a deep breath. "Byron used to date Ruth."

Virginia could barely contain her enthusiasm. Finally, someone who knew Ruth well, who would likely have met Matt, who might have some insight for her. She couldn't believe her luck.

"Please don't ruin this for me," Marney begged, and Virginia swallowed her smile and nodded.

They said their goodbyes and Virginia hurried home, late for work but feeling optimistic for the first time in a while. Finally, someone who might know something, and unlike Matt, she knew where Byron lived.

* * *

VIRGINIA ARRIVED home to find Lawrence mowing her lawn.

"What are you doing, mowing at this hour? You're going to get heat stroke."

Lawrence turned off the mower and wiped the sweat from his brow. "Last time I mowed in the morning, you yelled at me for disturbing your beauty sleep. Besides, it's barely April. Just wait until summer rolls in."

"Well, I owe you a cold drink for this," she said, unlocking her front door. "Oh, and I have gossip!"

When Lawrence had finished with her lawn, he came inside, sweating through his shirt and smelling of freshly cut grass. She used to love the way Earl smelled after mowing the lawn. Lawrence gripped the wall as he leaned over to take his shoes off before joining Virginia in the kitchen, where she handed him a glass of tea.

"Marney's got herself a boyfriend," Virginia said, grinning and raising her eyebrows. Lawrence was even more shocked than Virginia, and she reveled in passing along Marney's giddy description of their night out for dinner and anticipation of a second date, an evening of dancing at a new spot in the next town over.

"We should double date with them," she said, cuddling up next to Lawrence. He looked at her like she'd gone mad. "Oh, come on," she begged. "She seemed really serious about this guy. I want to spend some time with him, see if he's good enough for our Marney, but I can't just tag along like a third wheel by myself."

"There's something you're not telling me," Lawrence said, brow furrowed.

Virginia sipped her tea and shrugged. "I just think it would be a good time. And besides, maybe he has other handsome attorney friends he could introduce you to."

At this, Lawrence shook his head. "You know I'm done with all that."

"Pleeeease," Virginia pouted.

"Why do you want to spend time with Marney and her new beau so badly?"

Virginia sighed and lowered her voice. "Marney told me he used to date Ruth. I want to see if he knows anything, if he ever met Ruth's son, if he knew of anyone Ruth might have had it out with."

"Unbelievable." Lawrence set his glass down, shaking his head, and made to leave. "And here I thought you really cared about your best friend's first romance in ages."

"I do!" Virginia insisted, following him, but his words stung and a knot formed in her throat. "Please, Lawrence."

He turned to look at her and Virginia felt embarrassed. She'd truly been excited for Marney, but the moment a connection to Ruth turned up, she'd lost it.

Lawrence shook his head. "I've got to go. Thanks for the tea." He turned again to leave, and Virginia wished he'd slam the door behind him or act angry. Instead, he left her to sit alone in his disappointment, in her own shame.

And then, feeling so slimy she wanted to vomit, she picked up her phone and dialed Marney, put on a smile so it would carry through in her voice, and made plans to join her and Byron for lunch the next day.

* * *

WHEN VIRGINIA PULLED up at Bo's Biscuits, she felt her guilt slide away and make way for hope, hope that Byron would have information that helped her prove to the police that Ruth's death wasn't an accident. Even as the guilt disappeared, she wished it would return so she could at least tell herself she wasn't a horrible friend, that at least she felt bad about lying and secretly trying to interrogate her friend's first boyfriend in decades. She wanted to feel bad, knew she *should* feel bad, but she couldn't feel anything but a buzz of excitement.

Inside, the restaurant was lively but not packed. Businessmen in suits treated prospective customers to lunch, retirees finished up their brunches and card games and cleared out, freeing up a few tables, and college-aged kids with funky hair colors worked on laptops while sipping coffee at the bar.

Marney and Byron sat in a curved booth at the back corner of the restaurant, a neon sign above them depicting an anthropomorphic biscuit riding a skateboard. Virginia spied them first and waved, and Marney looked up and gave Virginia a beaming smile. Virginia felt a twinge of that guilt she'd wanted to feel earlier.

"Byron, this is my very best friend in the whole wide world, Virginia," Marney said as Virginia slid effortfully into the booth.

"It's a pleasure to meet you." He extended his hand and shook Virginia's. On his right hand he wore a class ring, its gold face standing out against his pale skin. He had gleaming blue eyes and bushy white brows to match the white frock of hair on his head.

"You as well," Virginia said. "Marney's told me a lot about you."

"All good things, I hope," he said with a laugh. He had a deep voice, powerful, though when he placed his hand on

though that's not what I anticipated when I went to law school. I loved it." He wore a wistful smile, and his eyes stared off into the distance.

"Why'd you quit? Marney said you worked part-time on pro bono cases after your official retirement. It sounds like you miss it."

The smile vanished from Byron's face, and he cleared his throat and took another sip of his drink. "It was just time," he said curtly. "But enough about the past. I like to focus on the now, embrace new hobbies, new reasons to wake up in the morning and try hard at something. Marney promised to teach me to crochet. Virginia, Lawrence, what do you like to do?"

"I bowl," Lawrence said, jumping into the conversation and looking grateful for the direction it had turned. "My team has won our league's championship half a dozen times. The Seaview Gulls."

"And Virginia gardens," Marney said, her voice dripping with pride. "You ought to see her place. The flowers are just remarkable. She's also part of the Garden Review Society. They go around and take pictures of local gardeners' pride and joy, then write up a review for the town. It's always so exciting for whoever they feature."

Virginia said, "I actually just told Gemma last week about the Breeze Village gardens and I think the *Review* is going to feature them in an upcoming issue. We've never featured a garden with multiple contributors like this, but some of the members are really excited."

Marney cooed in excitement, and Virginia wondered whether Marney was excited about the garden review or excited that Virginia was willingly expanding her ties to Breeze Village beyond questioning residents about Ruth.

Hating herself for it, Virginia exhaled and turned to Byron. "I really appreciated the gardens during Ruth's memorial service in the courtyard last week. Did you go?"

Byron squirmed uncomfortably and took a sip of his drink. "No, I didn't."

Virginia cocked her head to the side as if confused. "Didn't you date Ruth? I would have thought a former lover would want to be at her memorial. Did the relationship end badly?"

"Virginia," Marney chided, kicking her under the table.

Lawrence cut in to change the subject, but Virginia dug her heels in.

"Did you ever meet Ruth's son while you were together?"

Byron answered that he'd rather not talk about it, but Virginia kept pushing. She said he seemed like a most devoted son, but it was clear not everything was what it seemed. At this, Byron pushed his chair back and stood up.

"I'm not here to be interrogated." He nodded to Lawrence and said it was a pleasure to meet him, then apologized to Marney and turned and strode confidently from the restaurant. Marney shot Virginia a look of disdain and then hurried after Byron, leaving Virginia and Lawrence alone at the table.

Lawrence shook his head at Virginia but said nothing, leaving her to sit in her shame in silence. The teal-haired waitress returned with their plates, confused by the now empty seats where Marney and Byron had been.

"Something's come up," Lawrence said, flashing her a reassuring smile. "Would you mind boxing these up?"

Lawrence paid for their meals and handed Virginia the styrofoam box containing her lunch, then, without a word, left the restaurant carrying the others.

CHAPTER 14

On Friday, Virginia reluctantly donned a cropped pair of linen pants and a chambray button-down and adorned her ears and wrists with the flower-themed jewelry she wore to all her garden reviews. A pair of daisy earrings dangled from her earlobes and charm bracelets with dozens of gardening charms jingled and clanked on her wrists. The charms were all gifts, mostly from the gardeners of Seaview who had been grateful to the Garden Review Society for featuring their pride and joy. Though Gemma was the society president, Virginia had started the group and cultivated relationships with the gardeners in town. While Gemma would coordinate the visits, Virginia still arrived early to many a visit to help weed or prune or otherwise prepare, and the featured gardeners appreciated her for it.

Since she had been the one to suggest the Breeze Village gardens for the *Review*, she couldn't very well skip the visit, but she crossed her fingers that she would somehow avoid Marney. She still hadn't reached out to apologize after the lunch with Byron.

At Breeze Village, she met Gemma, Dorothea, and a few other members of the Garden Review Society in the lobby. They were animated in their discussion of whether they should feature Breeze Village or try to bring new blood into the society by featuring younger members of the town.

"When's the last time we featured a garden by someone under the age of sixty-five?" a portly woman was asking, her gingham overalls embroidered with the letters GRS for the Garden Review Society. "Our featured gardeners have been getting older and older, and now we're featuring a retirement community?"

"It's not our fault the seniors of Seaview are the ones with gardens worth reviewing," a woman with wild grey hair and turquoise glasses retorted.

"Good morning," Virginia interrupted their debate. "Ellen, I hear you, and for the next issue of the *Review*, I was thinking there's a community garden in that hippy neighborhood on the eastside that might be worth looking at. It's different from what we normally do, but it might attract a younger audience."

Ellen crossed her arms over her chest but didn't protest, and Gemma wrapped Virginia in a hug, the heavy scent of her perfume filling Virginia's nostrils.

"You're here!" Gemma's enthusiasm was as pervasive as her perfume. "Let's get started!"

Virginia led the half dozen other society members through the lobby, dining room, and out into the court-yard. The women spread out, fawning over the beautiful flowers and talking with the members of the Breeze Village garden club who were waiting to show off their work. Virginia smiled, though she still found herself nervously scanning the courtyard for signs of Marney. She turned to look back toward the main building and froze on the spot.

There was the woman from the office. Genie, Marney had said her name was.

Virginia's stomach clenched and she felt a coldness wash over her. Her mouth opened in surprise, but her throat was closed fast and she said nothing as the small, wiry woman made her way toward Virginia. She was, once again, dressed in all black, with her ornate cane in hand, thumping the ground with every step.

"Am I late?" the woman asked. Her voice was powerful and seemed almost out-of-place coming from her small, frail-looking body. She had the accent of a Southern aristocrat.

"I'm sorry?"

"For the Garden Review Society visit." She extended her hand, and Virginia eyed it before offering her own. Genie squeezed it, her grip as strong as her voice. "I'm Genie. I'm one of the garden club members here."

"Oh, of course," Virginia stammered and introduced Genie to Gemma, who immediately began asking questions about how frequently the club met, how they chose what to plant where, and whether there was ever any drama or difficulty cultivating a garden with so many people and their different opinions.

Genie answered Gemma's questions and the two seemed to be getting on well, so Virginia drifted off toward the other side of the courtyard. The still air felt humid, and Virginia hoped the spring shower predicted for that afternoon would hold off until she could get home. Otherwise, she'd be stuck at Breeze Village all day and would almost certainly have to confront Marney. A low, throbbing pain crept into Virginia's left hand and wrist, and she pulled a bottle of painkillers from her purse and shook one out into her open palm.

"What's the matter?"

Virginia jumped, dropping the pill onto the dirt, and spun around. Her heart beating wildly, she found herself face-to-face once again with Genie.

"I didn't mean to startle you. I just wanted to come over and thank you. Gemma told me it was at your suggestion that the Garden Review Society agreed to include our gardens in your next issue."

Virginia nodded absentmindedly, shaking another pill into her palm, this time successfully popping it into her mouth and swallowing it.

"What ails you?" Genie asked.

"Oh, just arthritis. It gets especially bad in the spring, what with the changing weather."

Genie nodded in understanding but said nothing.

"Look, about the other night," Virginia began. She hoped Genie would wave it away and tell her to forget about it, but instead, the woman looked at her expectantly. "I, err, I won't tell anyone."

"Tell anyone what? That you were snooping around in the patient files?"

"I just meant..." Virginia didn't know what to say, and Genie just continued to look at her with pursed lips and raised eyebrows, as if daring her to continue. Virginia sighed. "You know how that woman died a couple of weeks ago? Ruth?"

Genie nodded once.

"I just have this feeling it wasn't an accident. I ran into her son during the memorial and he was acting suspicious, but when I talked with the police, they didn't take me seriously. I hoped that if I could find his address, I could scope him out a little myself, find something to convince the police to look into him."

"You think Matt murdered his mother?"

"You know him?"

Genie shrugged as if it were obvious. "I'm Ruth's neighbor. Our rooms are right across the hall from each other, and Matt visits—well, visited—her all the time. I've met him once or twice when he came to visit, and Ruth talks—err, talked—about him all the time to anyone who would listen."

Virginia furrowed her brow. "And you think it's unlikely he killed Ruth?"

"Unlikely?" Genie let out a laugh. "Impossible! Matt would never. Anyway, I don't buy this 'murder' idea, and I don't want to talk about it." She turned to leave, but Virginia stopped her.

She asked Genie whether she knew anything about Byron's relationship with Ruth since she lived across the hall and might have heard or seen something. Was it possible that their relationship had ended badly?

Once again, Genie shook her head vehemently. "Byron would never. Their relationship ended amicably." She turned again to leave, but Virginia pressed on.

"Can you think of anyone else? Besides Byron, the scorned ex-lover, or Matt, the son ready to cash in on his inheritance, I can't think of anyone who might have had a motive to kill Ruth."

Genie clucked her tongue. "I already told you I don't think she was murdered." Still, she paused and leaned her head to one side as if considering the idea. "If you're really intent on investigating, the only person I can think of is Ronald."

"Ronald, the poker champion?"

Genie nodded. "Ruth was the favorite to win the tournament until she suddenly died the day before the final round."

Virginia was unconvinced and said as much. "Winning the retirement home poker tournament doesn't seem like a strong enough motive for murder."

Genie lowered her voice. "The poker tournament had a grand prize of one thousand dollars. Now, you didn't hear it from me, but Ronald has been struggling to pay the rent here, and that thousand dollars was a welcome windfall for him."

"You think he'd kill for that?"

Genie just shrugged. "To avoid losing his home?" The woman turned and walked away. This time Virginia let her go.

She knew firsthand what it felt like to be on the brink of losing one's home. But to kill for it? Virginia stood rooted to the spot, feeling like her head was spinning, and when she looked up, she saw Marney sitting down to lunch in the dining room with Byron. She felt the blood rush from her face and turned around, hoping Marney wouldn't see her. Without saying goodbye, she hurried through the courtyard, making her way around back to leave instead of going through the main building.

"Virginia, where are you going?" Gemma called after her, but Virginia couldn't hear her over the ringing in her ears. Instead, she rounded the corner, turning out of sight, head swimming with questions.

CHAPTER 15

Virginia arrived at work on Monday still salty from her morning dip in the ocean. She'd forgotten to replace her watch battery and hadn't realized the time was off until she was running late and had to hurry to work without showering or eating breakfast. Her stomach grumbled at her as she looked over the doctor's schedule for the day and began pulling files to get them ready.

As she flipped through the files and began making notes for Dr. DiMarco, the bell above the door jangled. "I'll be right with you, Mrs. Jacobs," Virginia said, not looking up from her work. She inhaled deeply. An over-whelming apple cinnamon smell filled the air, and she looked up in surprise.

"Sorry," a man said, gripping the back of one of the waiting room chairs and holding his right foot above the floor. "I'm afraid I'm not Mrs. Jacobs." The man limped to the reception desk and gripped it, his knuckles turning white and his face pale. "I tripped on the stairs yesterday and thought it was no big deal, but this morning I can barely walk, and it's awfully swollen. I was hoping if I came in first thing, there might be an opening?"

Virginia looked from the injured man to a small girl standing a few feet behind him. She couldn't have been more than five years old. Her curly blond hair stuck out at all angles, and she swayed back and forth on her sparkly silver shoe-clad feet while feeding herself from a pink plastic bowl of oatmeal.

"Sorry," the man said again, following Virginia's gaze to the girl standing behind him. "This is my daughter, Eloise. I couldn't get a sitter at the last minute."

Virginia assured the man that it was no trouble at all and offered Eloise a big smile. She took the man's name and handed him a clipboard with forms to fill out, then rummaged in the cabinet behind her and pulled out a half-filled coloring book they kept on hand to offer patients' children while they waited. The little girl's face lit up, and she took the book with glee.

In the silent waiting room, as Virginia returned to her seat and scheduled the man for the next available opening, Virginia inhaled the apple cinnamon smell again and felt her stomach twist in a knot. Certainly, a sprained ankle and apple cinnamon oatmeal meant nothing. It was a doctor's office, after all. People came in with sprained ankles all the time, and it wasn't uncommon for patients to bring their children and give them snacks while they waited. Virginia told herself that this was positively nothing to worry about, and it certainly didn't mean Colleen's prediction about an upcoming move had any merit.

Still, she thought, better to go talk with Colleen again when she finished at the office. Her curiosity stayed with her long after the limping man and his oatmeal-eating daughter waved goodbye and left, and when she got into her car to head home, she instead turned left and headed toward Breeze Village.

As the main building came into view, Virginia's heart began to race. The pale blue siding peaked through the tall oak trees, and the palms lining the crisp white front door appeared in her view. Palms sweaty, she watched as the driveway approached, then passed by as she missed the turn. Torn between turning around and pulling into Breeze Village to visit with Colleen or heading home to microwave another lasagna and eat it in front of the television, she took a deep breath and turned around.

Approaching Breeze Village from the other direction, however, she had an unobstructed view of the parking lot, and in the far corner of the lot, she spied a little white Mazda. She gasped. *Is that...?* An oncoming vehicle honked its horn and Virginia jumped, yanking the steering wheel to the right to avoid the headlights heading straight for her. Virginia exhaled once she was safely back in her lane, then returned her gaze to the parking lot where she now saw two pairs of eyes on her. There, in the far corner of the parking lot, half-hidden and tucked behind his car, Matt and Genie were looking her way.

"'I've met him once or twice,' my ass!" Virginia muttered to herself. She turned her attention back to the road, and when she looked back at the parking lot a moment later, Genie was gone and Matt's little white car was pulling out of the lot. She cursed under her breath and pushed down on the accelerator, determined to seize the opportunity to follow Matt, but before she could catch up with him, he turned onto a small side street and vanished.

* * *

PULLING UP AT BREEZE VILLAGE, still fuming after losing Matt, Virginia looked around for Genie, but she was nowhere to be found. She requested a visitor's badge, lying that she was there to see Marney and hoping they didn't call Marney to check with her, then walked down the hallway to where Genie's room stood across from Ruth's. Virginia heard noises coming from inside Ruth's room and wondered if someone new had moved into it already.

She was standing there, staring at Ruth's closed door, listening to the sounds from the other side, when a nurse came out of another room down the hall, startling her. She spun on her heel and knocked on Genie's door, but there was no answer.

Frowning, she turned and started back toward the lobby but stopped short when she saw the receptionist at the desk. Instead of risking having to explain why she wasn't heading toward Marney's cottage at all, she slipped into the stairwell and effortfully climbed the flight of stairs to the second floor before taking the elevator up one more level.

Virginia's heart pounded in her chest as she stood outside the elevator, gripping the railing that ran along all the walls in the main building and trying to slow her

err, I mean, I saw him at the store, and he was limping with a sprained ankle. He had his daughter with him, and she was eating apple cinnamon oatmeal. The other day, you mentioned an injured ankle and said you were overcome by the smell of apples and cinnamon. It just… it was just like you said."

Colleen smiled and nodded as if all this made perfect sense and was no surprise whatsoever. "I guess it wasn't just psychic interference at all. Still, not a very useful prophecy, was it?" She chuckled lightly. "Since you're here, would you like a reading?"

Virginia nodded, and Colleen bent over in front of a dark wooden desk with drawers up and down both sides.

"Let me just find the right deck," she muttered, pulling one knick-knack after another from the drawers before inspecting and replacing each in turn.

Finally, she stood and said, "Aha!" before taking a seat opposite Virginia across the low coffee table. She shuffled the gold-edged cards in her ring-adorned hands, and while she shuffled, Virginia exhaled and tried to sound nonchalant. "Colleen, do you do readings for lots of the residents here?"

Colleen continued to shuffle the cards, then closed her eyes and rested her hand on the top of the deck as if trying to draw energy from the cards or infuse them with her own energy. Virginia wasn't sure which.

"Sometimes," she said, opening her eyes. "Not everyone is open to my spiritual gift, but some are." She laid the cards on the table, their backs purple with gold designs.

"Do you ever do readings for Genie?"

At the mention of Genie, Colleen straightened up and looked from the deck of cards up to Virginia.

"No, not really," she said, then shook her head. "Well, sometimes. She does come to visit me on occasion, yes."

"Are you two close?" Virginia asked, and Colleen shook her head more fervently.

"No, not close. I wouldn't say that." She flipped over the top card to reveal an upside-down illustration of a robed man standing before a table and holding a candle. "The Magician, reversed." Colleen looked up at Virginia, a vague frown on her face.

"Is that bad?" Virginia asked.

"No card is *bad*," Colleen said, "but some can warn us of impending hardships, losses, challenges, or areas where we need to make changes. This card, for example, can signify trickery, illusion, deception." She looked at Virginia as if waiting for a response, but Virginia sat quietly, the image of Matt and Genie conversing in the parking lot at the front of her mind.

"Let's flip another," Colleen said, reaching for the deck again, but Virginia cut her off.

"What about Ruth? Did you know her well?"

Colleen looked up, brow furrowed, and shook her head. "She didn't care for the wisdom the spirit realm has to offer."

"And her son, Matt? Did you ever meet him?"

At this, Colleen pulled her hand back from the cards and clasped her hands together in her lap. "I can't say I did. What's this about?"

Instead of answering the question, Virginia pressed on. "Have you ever seen Genie and Matt together?"

Colleen stood abruptly and looked down at Virginia on the loveseat. "I'm sorry," she said shakily, "but your questions are clouding my energy. I need to commune with the spirits in private. We'll have to finish your reading another time."

Virginia apologized and hefted herself from the loveseat before leaving Colleen's room. The beaded curtain rattled against the door as it slammed shut behind her, and Virginia stood stunned, wondering what Colleen knew that she didn't want to share. Her head was spinning as she looked back at the door, beaded curtain still spinning, and she gripped the railing along the wall as she started back toward the elevator.

IN THE ELEVATOR, Virginia's reflection stared back at her from the mirrored elevator doors. Her gray hair looked thinner and wispier than she remembered, and when she looked down at her hand on the railing, she noticed the spots of discoloration and bright blue veins visible through her thin, pale skin. When did she become *old*, she wondered? Old and without grandkids to spoil or a husband to take on cruises to Alaska. Old and alone, she thought, and as the elevator doors opened, all she wanted to do was find Marney and curl up together on the couch, maybe put on a fun movie and belly laugh and feel alive together.

The elevator chimed and the doors opened to reveal the lobby, where the sounds of a poker game concluding filled the space. Ronald sat at a full table in the dining room, scooping chips toward himself with both arms while the other players protested. Virginia recognized the small man in a wheelchair and the brightly lipsticked woman from the previous game.

"Mind if I join you?" Virginia asked.

Ronald looked her up and down with narrowed eyes and pursed lips before nodding. "I could go for a rematch after that game after the memorial the other day."

Virginia took a seat and Ronald dealt out the cards. She had a poor hand, and as each card in the center of the table was flipped, she knew she didn't stand a chance. When she folded, Ronald's eyes gleamed, and when he won, she was surprised he didn't boast. Instead, he quietly shuffled the cards with a smile on his face. The others cleared out after the game, and Virginia stuck her hand out for Ronald to shake.

"Good game," she said. "I was hoping to take you again, but it, quite literally, wasn't in the cards tonight."

Ronald laughed. "I suppose that's life."

Virginia winced, since she was only spending time in Breeze Village because of a resident's untimely death. A resident Ronald might have had a motive to kill, even if his seemed flimsier than those of Byron and Matt.

"And you are the poker champion here, isn't that right?"

Ronald nodded, his smile widening, revealing his few teeth. "That's right."

"Wasn't Ruth also in the tournament before she died?"

Ronald's smile fell. "She was," he answered. "What's that got to do with anything?"

"Isn't it true you've been struggling to pay the fees to

stay here in Breeze Village for a while and that the prize money from the poker tournament was your saving grace? That you would have been kicked out had you lost to Ruth?" The direct accusation shocked even Virginia as it tumbled from her mouth.

Ronald recoiled, any remnants of his previous smile completely gone now. "What are you suggesting?"

Virginia faltered, feeling guilty at Ronald's shocked look, wishing she could take it back.

"Are you suggesting I killed Ruth to win a poker tournament?" Ronald continued. When Virginia remained silent, Ronald asked, "Is this because we dated?"

"You dated Ruth?" Virginia asked.

"You didn't know?"

"I thought Byron was the one who dated Ruth."

"They dated before she and I got together," Ronald said.

Virginia sat back down, feeling like her head was spinning.

"It's true what they say about romance and retirement homes," Ronald added with a smile before his face became serious again.

Virginia smiled but continued to sit in silence. She wondered why Genie hadn't told her Ronald had a romantic history with Ruth, only that he was in danger of losing the poker tournament.

"So why'd you break up?" Virginia asked.

Ronald shrugged. "After Byron, Ruth had a hard time opening up, trusting anyone. I'm eighty-three. I'm not interested in playing games or chasing after someone who doesn't know what she wants."

"What do you mean, she had a hard time trusting people after Byron?"

Ronald looked around to make sure no one was listening, then lowered his voice. "Byron and Ruth broke up because he stole from her." Virginia's mouth hung open in surprise. "Ruth was so shocked and hurt, she called the bar association. Byron had retired, see, but he was still taking on vulnerable clients pro bono, and Ruth thought a thief shouldn't be in that position."

Virginia gasped. "That's why he fully retired recently?"

Ronald shrugged. "Retired, was forced out, whatever you want to call it."

Virginia's head was really spinning now. Genie had told her they'd broken up amicably. Now Byron's hesitance to talk about Ruth or the end of his career made sense, but why would Genie lie for him? Was Byron mixed up in whatever Genie and Matt were up to?

Virginia's mind went straight to Marney, so excited to have a new lover, and she felt the blood drain from her face.

"Thank you for the information," she said, standing as quickly as she could. "I apologize for the accusations."

Ronald shrugged as if it were no big deal, then gathered his things and started toward the elevator while Virginia moved in the opposite direction, out the French doors and across the courtyard toward Marney's cottage.

Rap rap rap. Virginia knocked furiously at the door, but there was no answer. *Rap rap rap.* She knocked again. Still no answer.

"Are you looking for Marney?" a small voice asked.

Virginia jumped and spun around to find the woman

Virginia had seen knitting on the porch before standing behind her. She wheeled her oxygen tank beside her, and her hand was over her chest like Virginia's startled jump had, in turn, startled the woman.

"I didn't mean to scare you," she said. "My name's Jane. I just saw Marney leave with Byron a few minutes ago. They were dressed real nice and smiling. Looked like they were heading out on a date."

Virginia thanked her, and the woman turned and continued on her way.

Virginia leaned against Marney's door to steady herself, then took three deep breaths, pulled out her phone, and dialed Marney's number as she hurried to her car.

CHAPTER 16

Marney's phone rang and rang as Virginia hustled across the courtyard, through the dining room and lobby, and out to her car.

"What's the rush?" someone called out behind her, but she didn't turn around.

Virginia's heart soared when Marney's voice finally answered, then plummeted. "You've reached Marney Richards. Please leave a message."

"Hey, Marney, it's Virginia, just calling to check in on you," Virginia said. The message was interspersed with heavy breathing, and as she climbed into her car and shut the door behind her, Virginia gave herself a minute to slow her heart rate before turning the key in the ignition and peeling out of the parking lot.

At every stoplight, Virginia tried calling Marney again, and every time she did, the phone rang through to voicemail. *At least it's not off.* If Byron were going to murder Marney and leave her in a ditch, he'd stomp the phone like they did in the movies, right? Virginia increased the pressure on the accelerator and shook her head, trying to replace the images of Marney dead on the side of the road with images of Marney having too much fun dancing to hear her phone ringing in her bag.

"Answer, answer, answer...."

Virginia pulled into the cracked asphalt parking lot at the Seaview bowling alley and had to park at the far end of the lot in one of three remaining empty spots. She wondered what everyone was doing here on a Monday night, and for a brief moment, the full parking lot and protests from her legs as she tried to hurry across the asphalt occupied the front of her mind before worry for Marney reclaimed its place there.

Across the bowling alley, Virginia saw Lawrence, striped team jersey boasting his name and the number 7. He had just bowled a strike, and he threw his hands up and exchanged high-fives with his teammates.

"Lawrence!" she yelled. A few heads turned her way, but Virginia ignored them as she scrambled across the room toward her friend. Lawrence turned around, and a look of confusion and concern spread across his face as Virginia approached.

"What happened?" he asked.

"It's Marney!" Virginia said, out of breath.

"Is she okay?"

"She's not answering her phone."

Lawrence's face fell, and he sat down in one of the plastic chairs facing the ball return, gesturing for Virginia to sit next to him. When he questioned why Marney not answering her phone was enough to send Virginia into such a frazzled state, Virginia recounted her day, leaving out the mention of her job at the doctor's office, instead saying she saw the injured man and his daughter while she was downtown doing some shopping. She recounted seeing Genie and Matt together when she returned to Breeze Village, how Colleen abruptly ended her reading when she asked whether Colleen had ever seen them together, and finally the news from Ronald that Byron's relationship with Ruth hadn't ended amicably as he and Genie had led them to believe.

"She's the reason he had to quit practicing law," Virginia repeated. "And he already stole from her. If he was willing to steal while they were together, what's he willing to do after she dumps him and tries to get him disbarred?"

Lawrence shook his head. "I see why you're worried, but I think Marney screening your calls after you interrogated her boyfriend at lunch is not cause for this much concern."

"After I interrogated her boyfriend *who might be a murderer*," Virginia retorted.

"Look," Lawrence said, holding both hands up, "I'll give Marney a call tonight to make sure she's okay. But for now, I think we should assume she's out having a nice time on a date with a man who may have made a mistake in the past, and she doesn't want to talk with you right now."

Virginia started to protest, but Lawrence held his hands up again and she sighed and agreed. The exhaustion of the day was coming over her, and she wanted to release some of her worry so she could go to sleep.

"You'll call me if you can't get through to Marney?"

Lawrence nodded, and Virginia stood up, feeling the relief of sharing her burden with her friend. As the panic left her, she turned her focus to her body and felt the toll the day had taken on her. Her legs ached and wobbled, her head felt heavy, and pain shot through her arthritic wrist. She dug in her purse for the bottle of painkillers and cursed when she couldn't find it.

"What's the matter?" Lawrence asked.

"It's nothing." Virginia stood up a little straighter, trying not to wince as pain coursed through her body. She hugged her friend goodbye and began making her way back through the bowling alley, this time hobbling and gripping tables and chairs to steady herself as she walked.

WHEN VIRGINIA WOKE the next morning, she felt tranquil after sleeping straight through the night, a rarity, then panic when she remembered Marney's going out on a date with a murder suspect and being unreachable. She reached for her phone, knocking her alarm clock off the bedside table in the process, and saw that she had a missed call and a voicemail from Lawrence.

"Hey, it's Lawrence. Just calling to let you know I got hold of Marney and she's safely back in her cottage after her date with Byron. She forgot her phone when they went out. I hope you're sleeping soundly and not out with a murderer, seeing as you're not answering your phone. Talk to you later."

Virginia frowned at his quip as she returned her phone to the nightstand and stepped into the bathroom. She knew she should be relieved—her best friend was safe—but she felt embarrassment and a twinge of anger rise up in her. Byron may not have murdered Marney last night, but he was still a suspect for Ruth's murder in Virginia's mind. Genie and Matt were involved, somehow, and for some reason, Genie didn't want Virginia to know about Byron's motive for killing Ruth.

She brushed her teeth and dabbed rouge onto her cheeks before slipping into a pair of cream-colored slacks and a colorful striped blouse. She decided she'd call Marney from work and apologize for the barrage of calls the night before and for her behavior over lunch with Byron. If she was going to stand a chance at convincing Marney that this man wasn't Mr. Perfect, she needed to get back on good terms with Marney first.

Work was going smoothly once again. There were no walk-ins, no-shows, or cranky callers taking out their bad mornings on Virginia over the phone, so Virginia was feeling good.

During a gap between patients, Dr. DiMarco walked over and leaned on the reception desk. "I have to say, you're doing remarkably well."

Virginia beamed up at him, basking in the compliment.

"I wasn't sure how this was going to go, but since you've joined me, things are flowing much more smoothly around here. I just wanted to tell you how much I appreciate having you here."

Virginia felt like she was floating lightly above the rest of the world as she shuffled into the small coffee nook to brew herself another cup. While the coffee brewed, she gave Marney a call and was surprised when her friend picked up after the second ring.

"Sorry I missed all your calls yesterday," Marney said.

"No, I'm sorry I called you a million times." She paused and breathed into the receiver. "And I'm sorry for interrogating your new beau over lunch. That was... I shouldn't have done it." She waited for Marney's response, heart pounding in her chest.

"An admission of wrongdoing from Virginia Harold Walker? I must be hearing things."

The two laughed, and Virginia felt a peace settling inside her until Marney asked her to meet for lunch.

"Err, I have plans already," Virginia lied. "I'm supposed to go over to Dorothea's. How about I come over for dinner?"

Marney agreed, and Virginia hung up the phone and returned her attention to her coffee, stirring in cream and sugar. The bell above the door jangled and Virginia called out, "Just a minute!" She finished preparing her coffee and took a sip, tossing the wooden stirrer into the trash before emerging from the recessed coffee nook to return to her desk.

"Do you have an appointment?" Virginia looked up at the woman standing in front of the receptionist and stopped, frozen in her tracks.

Marney turned to look at her, jaw hanging open in surprise. "What are you doing here?"

Virginia didn't know how to respond. Instead, she stayed where she was, feet heavy like cinder blocks, and said, "We don't have you on the schedule today."

Marney nodded and clutched her small turquoise

purse in front of her. "I don't have an appointment, but if there's an opening, I'd like to be seen."

"What brings you in today?" The guilt and panic over being caught in her lie made way for concern for her friend's health, and Virginia returned to her seat behind the desk, looking up at Marney's cool face.

"I'd rather discuss that with the doctor."

"Of course." Embarrassed, Virginia returned her attention to the schedule and let Marney know of an opening after the doctor finished seeing his current patient. Marney took a seat in the waiting room facing away from Virginia's desk, and Virginia busied herself organizing the massive filing cabinets, though she couldn't stop herself from turning to glance at Marney every so often.

When Marney eventually emerged from the exam room and made her way to the exit, Virginia couldn't stop herself from running after her friend.

"Marney, wait!"

"Why? So you can lie to me some more?" Marney spun on her heel and faced Virginia, standing on the sidewalk, fists clenched and eyes burning.

"I just... you need to be careful with Byron." Virginia knew how the words sounded as they fell from her lips, but she couldn't let Marney go without trying to warn her of what she'd learned.

Marney threw her hands up in the air. "This again? I'm tired of you trying to tell me how to live my life. You know, it's rich, you thinking you're entitled to everyone's secrets while you're keeping so many of your own."

Virginia recoiled at the sting of Marney's words while Marney turned and walked away. Virginia stared after her

"Mrs. Walker," the woman exclaimed, bright pink lipstick forming a sickly sweet smile. "Chelsea," she reintroduced herself and stuck out her hand.

"I remember," Virginia said a little too emphatically, looking down at Chelsea's manicured hand but not taking it.

"Of course you do! Anyway, I left a letter taped to your door when I thought I'd missed you. I came to give you an updated offer on your house."

"You can offer me more money day in and day out, but I'm not selling," Virginia insisted.

Chelsea laughed coldly. "More money? I'm afraid there's been a misunderstanding."

Virginia cocked her head to the side and waited for Chelsea to explain.

"You know they publish notices of foreclosures in the newspaper, right?" Virginia's eyes grew wide, and a sneer formed on Chelsea's face. "I guess your secret isn't so secret after all. So here's the deal: you can take our offer of fifty grand, or you can lose the house and I'll swoop in and get it even cheaper than that after the fact. Either way, it doesn't look like you'll be staying in this house much longer."

"I've got it handled," Virginia said, pushing past Chelsea and ripping the envelope from her door. "I've got a job. I'm going to get on a payment plan for the tax lien. There isn't going to be a foreclosure."

"You're 'going to' get on a payment plan? Like you were 'going to' pay the taxes in the first place?" Chelsea snickered.

Virginia repeated that she had it handled before

unlocking the door and stepping inside, slamming the door behind her. Inside, she leaned her back against the door and whispered to herself, "I'm a fighter." Though the property developer hadn't meant it as a compliment when she suggested Virginia would fight their plans to buy her home, Virginia repeated it under her breath, feeling strengthened with every repetition. "I'm a fighter," she whispered. "I'm going to solve Ruth's murder. I'm going to secure the reward money. I'm going to keep this house. And I'm going to shove it in that god damned developer's face."

CHAPTER 17

Virginia's throat felt tight and her stomach churned. After attempting to force down a bowl of cereal for dinner, she gave up and dumped it down the sink, then grabbed her car keys and headed out the door. Her anger at the property developer turned to anger at Genie, and Virginia wanted answers.

"I'm a fighter," Virginia repeated to herself in the driver's seat of her car after pulling into the Breeze Village lot. Dusk was falling, and the sunset peeked through the oak trees. Several residents sat in the rocking chairs on the large front porch, reading or knitting or just staring off into the distance. Virginia gripped the railing as she climbed the stairs, then approached the receptionist's desk. "I'm here to see Genie," she told the woman.

The receptionist gave her a quizzical look. "Visiting hours are over."

"I'm a close friend. She'll be happy to see me." When the receptionist didn't respond, Virginia added, "It won't take long. I'll be out of here before you know it."

The receptionist's small eyes looked Virginia up and down, and she pursed her lips and gave a small nod. "Just be quick, will you?"

Virginia donned her visitor's badge and strode across the lobby to the hall where she'd found Ruth's body almost three weeks prior. Her pulse quickened and goosebumps broke out across her body. She lifted her chin and tried to convince herself she was confident before making her way to Genie's door and knocking three times, hard.

The wait for Genie to answer the door felt like it took minutes, though it couldn't have been longer than fifteen seconds. Virginia could hear her heart beating and felt nervous to speak—she wasn't sure if it would come out as a croak or a yell, but she felt sure it wouldn't come out as normal conversation.

The door swung back to reveal Genie, her dark skin smooth and her hair twisted up in a chignon. She wore all black, as usual, and held her cane beside her. When she saw Virginia, her mouth curled up in a smile that felt surprisingly warm and friendly.

"Virginia, what a lovely surprise. Come in." She stepped back into the room and gestured for Virginia to enter. All the fight in Virginia fled immediately as she was met with Genie's unexpected hospitality. Before she knew what she was doing, she had crossed the threshold and was standing in Genie's small space. The room was brightly lit, modern furniture out of place among the beige carpet and matching beige walls. A sculptural lamp looked regal atop a sleek metal side table, and a print of a Rothko painting in three shades of orange hung above the neatly-made bed.

The door clicked shut, and Virginia startled and spun around to see Genie standing in front of the now-closed door. Her smile was still in place, but it took on a menacing quality, and Virginia berated herself for coming alone and not telling anyone where she was going.

"Can I get you something to drink?" Genie offered, crossing the bright room to the small kitchenette.

"A tea would be nice." Virginia hung back nervously.

"Sorry, I don't have any tea. I hate the stuff. Never drink it. How about a cocktail?"

Virginia nodded in response, and Genie returned with two martini glasses full of light amber liquid, swirls of lemon peel garnishing the rims. Virginia took one of the glasses but didn't take a sip.

"So, tell me," Genie said, taking a seat in a curved, high-backed yellow chair. "Why are you here?"

Virginia remained standing, awkwardly holding her glass but not drinking. She stuttered a bit before answering, "I just thought we got off on the wrong foot, and I wanted to smooth things over."

Genie raised her eyebrows. "I didn't think there was any animosity between us."

Heat rose in Virginia's face. Here Genie was, acting like they were friendly when she'd lied to her face in the gardens.

"I talked to Ronald," Virginia said.

"Ah, your investigation. That's what brings you here. You still think Ruth's death was something sinister?"

"Ronald and Ruth dated. You didn't think that was important to tell me when we were discussing potential motives?"

Genie shrugged. "It must have slipped my mind. Besides, Ronald has dated half the women in Breeze Village, and none of them have turned up dead."

"Do you know why Byron and Ruth broke up?"

"How long are you going to keep up this interrogation?"

"Until I find the truth. Do you know why Byron and Ruth broke up?" she repeated.

"No, I don't," Genie said, cocking her head to the side and looking at Virginia expectantly.

"He stole something from her and she tried to get him disbarred for it. She's the reason he went into full retirement."

Genie frowned. "That's unfortunate," she said simply.

Virginia's pulse quickened, and some of her unsipped cocktail sloshed onto the floor as she worked to steady herself.

"May I use your restroom?" she asked.

Genie pointed to one of two doors on the far wall, and Virginia set down her glass and slipped into the small restroom. Inside, she leaned against the counter, both hands gripping the pristine countertop as she leaned toward her reflection. Her heart thudded in her ear, and she tried to calm herself.

A minute passed, and Virginia looked around the restroom. The shower curtain, bathmat, and towels brought splashes of color to the room, contrasting the bright white floor and countertop. Nothing seemed amiss, and Virginia started to leave when she noticed the medicine cabinet. Without thinking, she pulled it open slowly and peered inside.

A gasp escaped her lips. There were more pill bottles than Virginia had seen in any one place except a pharmacy. Her stomach dropped and her head spun as she tried to think of reasons Genie might have so many pill bottles. She squinted to read the small print on the bottles, but without her glasses it was useless, and those were tucked away inside her purse next to Genie's door.

Heart racing, she left the restroom and walked swiftly to the door, picking up her purse. "I'm sorry, I have to go," she said, already halfway out the door.

Genie called after her, confused, but Virginia didn't turn around. Instead, she hurried down the hallway, through the dining room, which was empty save for one table occupied by a handful of residents working on a jigsaw puzzle, and then out into the courtyard. She passed Byron as she crossed the courtyard.

"Virginia, is everything all right?" he called to her, but she didn't stop. She'd question him later, but right now she needed her friend. She needed someone else on her side.

"VIRGINIA, WHAT ARE YOU DOING HERE?" Marney's initial surprise turned to a cold frown when she pulled open the door in response to Virginia's frantic knocks.

"It's Genie," Virginia huffed, out of breath.

"Is she okay?"

Virginia nodded and tried to wave away Marney's concern. "She's fine. It's just... I was just there, in her room, and I went to the bathroom, and I looked in her medicine cabinet—"

"Unbelievable," Marney cut her off. "You really can't help yourself, can you?"

"Marney, she had so many pill bottles. She's up to something."

"You don't think every resident of Breeze Village has a fully stocked medicine cabinet? We're old! We've got ailments out the wazoo! And pills to treat those ailments."

"No, this was different." Virginia shook her head vehemently. "I also saw Genie with Matt yesterday."

At this, Marney's anger faded, and a hint of curiosity crossed her face. She stepped out of the doorway so Virginia could come inside.

"Genie's up to something, and whatever it is, Matt's involved. Remember, I saw her sneaking around in the office? The office is attached to the nurses' station, which is practically a fully-stocked pharmacy. There's no way all those prescriptions in her cabinet are hers." A memory surfaced, and Virginia shouted, "Oh! And my painkillers went missing from my bag after talking with Genie at the Garden Review Society visit. She saw me take one and asked about them, and then the next time I went to take one, poof, they were gone."

Marney frowned slightly. Her voice was soft. "Virginia, you've lost prescriptions before. And there's a chance Genie is just more ill than anyone is aware of. Did you happen to see what all these mysterious pill bottles contained?"

Virginia shook her head. "I didn't have my glasses with me."

Marney sighed. "I can call Dylan."

"They'll just blow me off again," Virginia protested. "Dylan will send another officer because she's too busy with her other investigations, and that other officer will see two old ladies concerned about the number of prescriptions in another old lady's medicine cabinet and laugh all the way back to the station."

"What better idea do you have?"

Virginia and Marney stood in silence, Marney staring at Virginia and waiting for a suggestion and Virginia staring at her feet, wishing one would come to mind.

Eventually, Virginia sighed. "I'm sorry, by the way," she said, looking up to meet Marney's gaze. "For interrogating Byron. For lying to you."

Marney's face softened. "Why are you working at the doctor's office? And why didn't you tell me?"

"With you in Breeze Village, I needed something to pass the time," Virginia said, her stomach tightening at the lie. She wasn't ready to tell Marney yet about the yellow notice on her door, the impending foreclosure, the pink suit-clad woman trying to buy the house out from under Virginia for way less than it was worth.

"How much free time could you have, what with how hard you've been pushing this investigation?" Marney joked darkly. She sighed and looked up at Virginia and apologized.

"There's something else I need to tell you," Virginia said. "It's about Byron."

Marney started to protest, but Virginia put her hands up to stop her. She recounted what Ronald had told her about Byron's relationship with Ruth, how she was responsible for the end of a career he loved. As she spoke, Marney's mouth opened slightly and her eyes grew wide. Virginia thought she saw tears forming in them.

"We need his side of the story," Virginia said. "If Genie is trying to direct me away from Byron, maybe there's something he knows that she doesn't want us to find out. Some reason she doesn't want me asking him too many questions."

"Absolutely not," Marney said. "I won't involve him. A bad breakup and a theft—if that's even true—does not turn a good man into a murderer. And Byron is a good man. Besides, who's to say Ronald wasn't lying? Byron was his girlfriend's ex. No one likes their partner's exes. No, the only next step I can get on board with is to call Dylan and get the police involved."

"They won't believe me," Virginia argued. "They've already shown they don't take me seriously, and what do I even say to them? 'Oh, hi, Officer. A resident of a retirement community has a suspicious amount of pills in her medicine cabinet. No, I don't know what kinds of pills they are or have proof they're not hers, but I have a feeling she's up to something suspicious and illegal, and maybe she's even involved in the murder you don't believe was a murder.' I don't know if that'll go over well."

Virginia brought her hand to her mouth and bit at her fingernails, then pulled it away to stop herself. Finally, she said, "Okay, I'll agree to call the police, but not without some sort of hard evidence."

"Hard evidence?"

"I'm going to go back to Genie's room and get one of the pill bottles. Proof."

"No way!" Marney objected. "She could be dangerous."

"I thought you said she's just an ailing senior with a lot of prescriptions?" A playful smile crossed Virginia's face, and she turned and strode toward the door, opening it and stepping out into the cool night before Marney could protest further.

* * *

"VIRGINIA, WAIT!" Marney called out, trailing behind Virginia. She was quicker than Virginia, always had been more athletic, and Virginia focused all her energy on crossing the courtyard and getting to Genie's room. She'd make up an excuse, say she left something behind, and be in and out before Genie could react. Virginia cursed under her breath. It was a stupid plan, she knew. Though she was small, Virginia knew Genie wasn't weak or slow.

"Virginia!" Marney repeated, this time a hiss rather than a yell. "Okay, fine, you can go, but we at least need a plan!"

Marney caught up to Virginia and the two slowed, catching their breath on the patio before entering the main building. Through the French doors, they could see that the lobby was dimly lit, and both it and the dining room were empty. The chilly air whipped around them and made them shiver.

"I have a plan," Virginia said. "I'll tell Genie I dropped something when I was in the bathroom earlier and go in there to get it."

"I thought you didn't take anything into the bathroom with you?" Marney questioned.

"I'll be quick," Virginia insisted. "She won't have time to object."

Marney shook her head but didn't argue. "At least let me come with you. I can distract Genie to make sure you get a minute alone in the bathroom."

Virginia reluctantly agreed, and together they made their way through the empty dining room and into the lobby, the light clicks of their shoes on the linoleum floor the only sounds. They turned down the hallway where Genie's room sat opposite the room that was Ruth's, but stopped in their tracks.

In the middle of the hallway, a person lay sprawled on the floor.

"Are you okay?" Virginia called hesitantly. She crept toward the mass, Marney close behind her, but when they got closer they could see that the person was not okay.

There, lying in a pool of blood, was Byron.

Marney cried out and stopped, frozen to the spot about six feet away from Byron's body. Virginia gripped the railing along the wall, suddenly dizzy and nauseated. How had this happened? She'd seen him not ten minutes earlier, crossing the courtyard. She'd been standing in the very place he lay just moments before that.

Byron's head and face were covered in blood, the source of the pool on the carpet. Virginia tore her eyes from his body and looked up, mouth agape. Her stomach fell as she realized where in the hallway they were. They were standing directly outside Genie's room, the door ajar in front of them.

"Genie?" Virginia called, creeping around Byron's limp body and toward the partially opened door. There was no answer. Virginia called out again and then poked her head inside the door, slowly opening it the rest of the way.

Inside the room, Genie lay face down on the floor, beaten over the head the same as Byron had been. A sleek, rectangular lamp shade lay on its side on the floor beside the bright yellow chair Genie had sat in earlier that evening, but the lamp base was missing.

Virginia's head spun, and she stumbled backward into a small side table, toppling a picture frame. She turned and caught herself before staggering back out into the hallway, where she clasped the railing again to keep from falling over. A ringing in her ears blocked out Marney's crying, and she hardly noticed the doors opening down the hall, residents looking to see what the commotion was about.

"Stand back!" a voice shouted, and Virginia turned to

see the nurse, Haley, rushing toward them. She dropped to her knees in front of Byron's body, turning him over and checking for a pulse Virginia knew she wouldn't find. She spoke into a radio she carried and then moved quickly to Genie's body, repeating the process. Virginia watched as Haley turned Genie over onto her back and placed her fingers on Genie's neck before speaking into her radio again.

More staff flooded the area, and Virginia and Marney were pushed back down the hallway and eventually into the dining room where they sat, stunned, and waited. This time there was no talk of an accident. Genie and Byron had been murdered, and Virginia and Marney would need to give their statements.

Staff flitted in and out of the hallway until police poured in and blocked it off. Residents were asked to stay in their rooms for the time being.

"Mom!" a familiar voice rang out, and Virginia and Marney looked up to see Dylan rushing toward them. "What happened?"

Dylan wrapped Marney in an embrace and held her while she cried. When Marney had caught her breath, Dylan crossed the room and brewed two cups of tea, then brought them to the table where Marney and Virginia sat.

"Are you going to be the one taking our statements?" Virginia asked.

Dylan shook her head and stood, apologizing, then held out her arm, gesturing to an officer who was standing off to the side before introducing him as Detective Kincaid. Virginia was relieved to see that it wasn't Officer Matthews, the dismissive officer she'd spoken to

"I'm going to head back," Marney said, gesturing toward the doors to the courtyard. "Stay the night?"

Virginia shook her head. "I want to sleep in my own bed tonight."

The two exchanged goodbyes, and Virginia watched Marney walk through the French doors and out into the courtyard. She turned to leave through the front doors but paused in the eerie silence. The receptionist had gone home, the police and the medical examiner had left, the bodies had been removed, and now what remained was an empty hallway with a stain on the carpet blocked off with caution tape.

Before she even knew what she was doing, Virginia found herself pacing quietly down the hallway, then ducking under the bright yellow tape blocking off the middle portion of the hallway and Genie's room.

ALONE IN THE EMPTY SPACE, Virginia peered down at the stained carpet, tape outlining where Genie's body had laid earlier that evening. An identical scene lay in the hallway just outside the door, outlining where Byron had been. Virginia had seen them both just minutes before their deaths, had been in this very room, frightened of Genie, had pushed past Byron on the way to Marney's cottage to describe what she'd found in the medicine cabinet.

A tear slipped down Virginia's face, and she shook her head, trying not to think of how quickly things had changed. She strode to the bathroom and gasped when she found the medicine cabinet entirely empty. Nothing else in the room seemed to have been touched. In the living room, evidence markers indicated places where police had removed evidence from the premises. Virginia looked in the medicine cabinet again. Empty.

Virginia's head spun as she emerged from the bathroom. She knew she hadn't imagined the pill bottles before, but how had they just disappeared?

As she made to leave the room, eager to get away from the grim scene, something caught Virginia's eye: a styrofoam cup of tea sitting on the bookshelf beside Genie's chair. The cup was full and the tea bag was still inside. It appeared untouched. Genie never drank tea, Virginia knew. She didn't even keep it in her room. So why was it here?

Ruth had supposedly died of an accidental overdose, but Virginia had suspected that someone else had given her the medications. Now Virginia wondered whether that person had tried to do the same to Genie.

* * *

SHE PICKED up the cup and started to leave the room. There had to be some way to find out what was in this tea. Her mind went to the lab at work, the little cups of urine she boxed up for them to take at the end of each day. Maybe she could fill one of those cups with the tea and have it tested? Or bribe a newbie to test it for her?

Lost in thought, Virginia startled when she reached the dining room and heard voices. She looked up from the mug in her hands and was surprised to see Haley sitting with a resident, both eating chocolate pudding cups.

"Can I help you?" Haley asked, setting hers down and standing up. She eyed the visitor's badge still hanging from Virginia's neck but didn't mention it. Her fake eyelashes had held up strong, but eyeliner had formed dark circles under her eyes, and Virginia was shocked to see that Haley was still wearing the same scrubs from earlier, bloodied from when she'd turned the bodies over before the police arrived.

"No, I was just leaving." Virginia started to turn toward the door to the parking lot when the resident sitting with Haley spoke up.

"Who are you?" she demanded in a hoarse voice.

"Mom," Haley hissed. She turned to Virginia with an apologetic look. "This is my mom, Midge. She just moved into Ruth's room a few days ago. It's nice having her so close, but at the same time... Anyway, I'm very sorry you've had such a traumatic evening."

"Ruth's room? Across from Genie's?"

Haley nodded.

"Did you see or hear anything tonight, then? Anything suspicious?"

Haley shook her head no. "I already talked with the police. What a shame. You'd think I'd have heard something being right there, maybe even been able to glimpse the perpetrator. But no."

"My daughter is the reason I'm here, you know," the older woman croaked.

Virginia turned and started to ask what she meant, but Haley shushed her mother and insisted it was time to get her to bed after the chaos of the evening. She took the nearly finished pudding cup from Midge's twisted hands and placed it on the table before stepping behind her and gripping the handles of her wheelchair. Haley bid Virginia goodnight and began to wheel Midge toward the hallway, and Virginia wondered how they'd get in and out of her room without wheeling right over a crime scene.

"Drat!" Virginia's thoughts were interrupted as Haley cut the turn too tight and bumped Virginia with the wheelchair, knocking the cup of tea out of her hand and spilling it on Virginia's clothes and onto the floor.

"I am so sorry!" Haley apologized profusely, but didn't stick around to assess whether Virginia was all right. Instead, she continued wheeling her mother down the hall, leaving Virginia wet and alone to process the loss of the one piece of evidence that could connect Genie's and Byron's murders to Ruth's death.

CHAPTER 19

Neither the clock, the sun streaming in through the curtains, nor Virginia's bladder tore her from her bed before noon Wednesday morning. It had been late by the time she'd arrived home and fallen into bed with barely enough energy to strip off her clothes and don pajamas first. When she finally stirred, she felt disoriented. The room was too bright, and her eyes felt heavy and dry. She was still out of it by the time she left her bedroom, robe wrapped around her, and noticed the voices coming from her kitchen.

"Hello?" she called.

Lawrence poked his head out of the kitchen and greeted her with a smile. "Your kids came over." Though he said it happily, Virginia knew it was a warning so she would have time to collect herself before entering the kitchen.

"Coming home to find you kids here without my knowing is becoming a bit too frequent," Virginia said as she crossed into the cramped kitchen, smiling though she

153

was annoyed and discreetly palming a sticky note on the counter reminding her to take out the garbage.

"You finding dead bodies is becoming a bit too frequent," Lucy joked.

Jack's eyes grew wide, and he elbowed his sister, telling her to cut it out, but Virginia cracked a genuine smile at the joke before remembering the scene from the night before and gripping the counter to steady herself as a wave of nausea passed over her.

"So, what food did you bring me this time?" Virginia asked, trying to act casual and force the vision of Byron's limp body and the sounds of Marney's cries out of her head.

Jack eyed her, not buying it, before telling her they'd ordered delivery from her favorite Italian place. "It should be here in twenty minutes."

Virginia poured herself a cup of coffee, grateful that if her children were going to be invading her space without warning, at least they knew her well enough to brew coffee for her. She wondered if it had been the kids or Lawrence who made the pot of coffee and looked over at her friend, who shot her an apologetic glance.

"Look," Jack said, catching Virginia's attention. "I know you're fine. Or, I know you'll say you're fine. But what happened last night, and what happened almost three weeks ago, was traumatic. It's something no one should have to go through, and you've had to go through it twice in a month." He exhaled like he was preparing himself to say something difficult. "I'd like you to see a therapist."

Silence fell in the crowded kitchen. Virginia stared at

Jack with narrowed eyes, as if silently asking him if he were serious. Lucy and Lawrence looked from Virginia to Jack and back, eyes wide, waiting for Virginia's explosion. When none came, they seemed pleasantly surprised, if still a little nervous. Jack turned to the table behind him and picked up a small binder, holding it out to Virginia. At this, Virginia couldn't hold it in any longer.

"Another binder?" She looked from Jack to Lucy and Lawrence. "Are you two in on this?"

Lawrence shook his head aggressively and held his hands up in front of him, indicating he had no involvement.

Lucy grimaced and said, "I don't think it's a terrible idea."

"Have you forgotten that the last time you handed me a binder trying to tell me how to live my life, I kicked you out?"

At this, Lucy walked over and took the binder from Jack, hugging it to her chest and giving Virginia a pleading look. "Dylan is recommending the same thing to Marney. She called this morning to ask us how you were." She narrowed her eyes and gave Virginia a scathing look. "How surprised she was to hear that we didn't even know what had happened. She had the pleasure of informing us that our mother was the first one to come across a brutal murder scene."

Virginia folded her arms across her chest and ignored the pointed look she could feel coming from Lawrence. No, she hadn't told them, but she was going to. At least, that's what she told herself. For Pete's sake, she'd only just woken up. When was she supposed to have told them?

"It's not just the one traumatic incident," Jack said. "With all the changes going on in your life, it just might be helpful to have someone to talk to. Someone you're more comfortable sharing with than us."

Thinly veiled hostility underlay the statement, but Virginia paid it no mind.

"What do you mean, all the changes in my life?" They'd learned about the murder scene before she'd told them. Was it possible Chelsea had looked them up to get them to talk her into selling?

Lucy put her hand on Virginia's elbow. When Virginia yanked it away, she saw the hurt in Lucy's eyes and looked down at her slipper-clad feet, ashamed at how closed off she was from her own children.

"Just, with Marney moving into Breeze Village, and now two major incidents just a few weeks apart, it's a lot," Lucy said.

A knock at the door interrupted their conversation, and the door swung open to reveal Jack's wife Stephanie holding up two paper bags of food and grinning. "I intercepted the delivery guy in the yard." Stephanie stepped inside and made her way to the kitchen, and though the small room was now more cramped than before, Stephanie's bubbly energy dissipated the tension and made it feel less crowded.

Virginia accepted a tin container of pasta from Stephanie and looked her over. She wore her usual paint-covered overalls, hair tied up in a bun with a dark blue scarf wrapped around her head like a headband.

"How's work going?" Lawrence asked Stephanie as he dished lasagna from a tray onto his plate.

She beamed as she described a gallery showing she was preparing for. "We're two weeks out, so of course I'm over-caffeinated and under-rested, but flying high all the same." She always seemed to be flying high, and Virginia wondered how bubbly, energetic, free-spirited Stephanie had found her way to Jack, the accountant who prepares binders for every life decision. Opposites attract, she supposed, and she was glad they'd found each other.

"Stephanie," Virginia turned and smiled at her daughter-in-law, "do you think I need therapy?"

Stephanie's smile drooped a tad, and she looked from person to person before settling back on Virginia and clearing her throat. "Need? I'm not sure." Virginia raised her chin and gave Jack a triumphant look. "But I think it's probably a good idea and certainly worth trying, in the aftermath of something so awful."

"That's it, you're out of the will!" Virginia joked.

Lawrence asked Stephanie more about her upcoming gallery showing. Jack and Lucy conversed about their jobs and neighborhood scandals. Virginia ate her food in silence, wondering whether Marney would accept Dylan's recommendation and go to therapy. If Virginia had just taken one of those pill bottles when she first saw them, Marney wouldn't be in this position at all. They wouldn't have gone back, and they'd have slept peacefully and learned of the murders the next day along with the other residents.

Of course, had they not been on the scene, Virginia wouldn't have seen the cup of tea, wouldn't have known the pill bottles disappeared with no police evidence marker. Virginia hated herself for it, but she thought it was almost worth it. She had more of the puzzle pieces to understanding Ruth's death and the connection to Genie and Byron than ever. She just had to figure out how to put them together.

* * *

THE NEXT TEA party for the ladies of Grove Park was at Sue's house, and when Virginia arrived, a tray of finger sandwiches in hand, the first thing she noticed was the presence of mobility aids scattered around Sue's house. She'd never seen Sue use a cane or a walker, but here at her home she had non-slip mats and grip bars placed around the house. Virginia wondered if her children were trying to push her into a retirement home or if they trusted Sue to know what she needed.

"Come in!" Sue took the dish from Virginia's hands and ushered her inside. When Virginia asked whether she'd installed the grip bars and aids herself or had someone come do it, Sue beamed and said her daughter had installed them for her. Virginia cringed at the thought of what Lucy and Jack would say if Virginia admitted to needing modifications around the house.

"Just the woman I've been looking for!" Virginia turned to see Dorothea standing before her. She was wearing a colorful beaded blouse made of a silky butter-fly-patterned fabric. Beaded fringe hung from the bottom of the blouse and tapped against her pale pink slacks as she gestured when she spoke. "I have not been able to stop thinking about you and your investigation! Have you cracked it and claimed the reward money yet?"

Virginia gave a small smile. She was conscious of all the eyes on her as the rest of the neighbors quieted down and moved into the living room where Virginia and Dorothea were standing. "Not yet," Virginia said quietly. Then, when she saw several women frown with disappointment and turn back to their previous conversations, she couldn't help herself and continued, "But there has been a new development. Two more murders at Breeze Village, just this week."

The living room was now full as every guest moved closer to hear what Virginia had to say. She recounted her suspicions of Genie and Matt, the sheer number of prescription bottles in Genie's cabinet, and finally, her and Marney's discovery of the bodies. When she reached this point of the story, Virginia surprised herself and her audience with a sob.

"I'm sorry," Virginia apologized and looked around her for an escape route, suddenly uncomfortable with all the eyes on her. An escape was not to be had, as the women she'd known for decades closed around her, wrapping her in a hug and comforting her.

When she was released, Dorothea put a hand on Virginia's shoulder. "You think these murders are connected to that other woman's death last month?"

Virginia nodded. "I know they are."

"Good. You're a good detective, Virginia. You knew something was out of sorts before the police did. Don't let up on this." Dorthea's plump hand gripped Virginia's shoulder, and Dorthea nodded to punctuate her point before letting go and turning to pour herself a cup of tea. Virginia's stomach tightened at the sight, and she wondered what the next step was now that the only piece of evidence that might tie the two events together had been sloshed on the floor.

Virginia accepted a cup of punch instead of tea and fixed herself a small plate of sandwiches, fruit salad, and petit fours.

Behind her, Sue said, "I sure am glad I've got kids with a mother-in-law suite so I've got a place to go that's murder-free."

"I'm on the Breeze Village waitlist," Gemma said. "I'm not worried about it, and I've heard the food there is great. I'll take my chances to avoid cooking for myself ever again."

"I'm moving into Harbor Vale in three weeks," Jan piped up.

Virginia frowned and furrowed her brow. "Why is everyone suddenly talking about moving?"

"It's that developer woman who's been coming around buying up all our houses," Kim said, giving Virginia a questioning look. "Hasn't she come to you?"

Virginia nodded slowly and said she had, but that the offer had been insultingly low. "So you all agreed to sell your houses? Half of you have been here your whole lives like I have."

Sue shrugged. "The offer was fair, and I've been feeling the need to downsize. It's been harder and harder to keep this place clean lately, and you see all the contraptions I need to get around by myself and feel safe." She gestured around at the mobility aids.

Virginia turned to face Kim. "And you sold, too?" Kim nodded. "Where are you moving to?"

"I found a little bungalow on the south side, closer to my kids."

"I thought you said you'd never move? You were committed to staying where you were?" Virginia fought to keep from raising her voice, but she felt like the floor had been pulled out from under her.

Kim simply shrugged and gave Virginia a smile. "One must look out for one's own interests." Heat rose in Virginia's face, and she took a sip of punch to avoid saying something she'd regret.

After a few deep breaths, Virginia asked, as calmly as she could, though her voice still shook, "How many of you agreed to sell?"

Two-thirds of the dozen women packed in Sue's small living room raised their hands, and the others muttered about being in negotiations or trying to get a better deal, but none of them seemed to be planning on staying. Of course, the developer had been talking to everyone, but it hadn't crossed Virginia's mind until now. She set her plate down on the coffee table, unable to eat with the knot forming in her stomach.

"Are you trying to negotiate a higher price out of them?" Kim asked Virginia.

When Virginia shook her head and said she'd flat refused to sell, Jan looked like Virginia had just said she was jumping out of an airplane without a parachute.

"One of my friend's nephews tried fighting Bellemeade a few years ago," she said. "They took his house for pennies compared to their initial offer and made his life hell while they were fighting. I wouldn't fight them if I were you."

Virginia frowned, then looked up at Kim. "They're talking to the whole neighborhood, right?" Kim nodded. "I've got to go," Virginia said suddenly, standing and making her way to the door, leaving her half-eaten plate and a dozen stunned women in her wake.

WHEN VIRGINIA STRODE up to her house, just two blocks from the tea party underway at Sue's, Lawrence was standing in her yard, pruning the bushes that lined the front of her house. Virginia stood on the concrete path, and Lawrence, sweating even in the cool morning air, looked up at her.

"Something wrong?" he asked.

Virginia shook her head but glowered at him when he looked down and continued working.

After a moment, he looked back up at her and asked, "Really, what's wrong?"

"The sandwiches weren't great this morning. I'm just hungry," Virginia said. She started toward the front door and Lawrence nodded and went back to work shaping the bushes, stepping back to eye his handiwork. Virginia felt rage rise up inside her. How could he just pretend nothing was happening in their neighborhood?

She stopped in the middle of the path and waited for Lawrence to pause and look up at her again. "Did you sell out, too?" she yelled when she had his attention.

Lawrence's hands dropped to his sides and he gave Virginia an apologetic look. "I knew we'd have to have this conversation eventually."

CHAPTER 20

As the ocean water lapped at Virginia's skin, her body drifting with the undulating currents, Virginia eyed the shore and the buildings beyond, wondering which window might be Lawrence's someday. Which building, which balcony, where would he go when he left her? The tears that rolled down her face mixed with the salty water, and she tipped her head back, floating on the surface as the rise and fall of the waves comforted her like a mother rocking her child.

All night, Virginia had lain awake thinking of her options. She could sell her house to Chelsea for a fraction of what it was truly worth and never speak a word of what went into the decision to Lawrence, Marney, or her children. She'd have a hard time affording somewhere else to live without getting a good value for her current home, but she could probably find something north of town that might work. She could admit to her children that she needs help to avoid foreclosure but then still end up selling her house to Chelsea and the rest of the Bellemeade bandits so hellbent on buying up her neighborhood. At least that way, she could negotiate to get a fair price for it. She could solve the Breeze Village murders and hope Dorothea was right about the reward money. That would keep her from having to tell anyone about the impending foreclosure, but it wouldn't keep Bellemeade from making her life hell until she sold them her home.

The more she turned the options over in her head, the more she thought letting the current carry her out to sea sounded like the best choice. Even if she managed to get a fair price from Bellemeade, where would she go? Gemma had mentioned a waitlist for Breeze Village. Virginia wondered how long it was. The idea of capitulating to her kids' desires and moving into a retirement home without even being able to be in the same one as Marney was unbearable. When she tried to picture herself tending to another home besides the one she'd known her whole life, she couldn't.

Virginia ducked down under a wave, and when she finally put her feet down on the sandy ocean floor and stood, she felt newly calm and grounded. Bellemeade was going to fight her no matter what, but the foreclosure was the more immediate concern. Faced with the choice to give up and lose the house, confess to her children that she needed help, or play detective and solve a series of murders the police didn't seem to be making headway on, the latter seemed like the best option. And so Virginia kicked off from the sand and caught a wave, body surfing to the shore, and emerged feeling confident in her next steps: she needed to get into the police station and find out what they knew.

* * *

AFTER WORK, Virginia drove straight to the station, her pulse quickening the closer she got. Having been dismissed repeatedly when she tried to point out her suspicions around Ruth's death, she braced herself for another instance of being treated as a senile old woman who had nothing of value to say, reminding herself that her primary purpose on this mission wasn't to be listened to but to find out what the police knew.

Though Dylan had been an officer for twenty years, Virginia hadn't ever stepped foot inside the police station. When she stepped through the double doors, she was met with a small lobby where a reception desk was protected by plastic walls and a few uncomfortable-looking benches sat off to the side. A nervous man sat on one of the benches, crossing and uncrossing his legs repeatedly and looking from his lap to the door and back.

"Hello," Virginia said, approaching the reception desk. Her voice wavered and she cleared her throat. "I'm here to see Dylan Richards."

The woman behind the desk didn't look up at Virginia. "Do you have an appointment?" she asked, not taking her eyes off her computer screen.

When Virginia said she didn't, the woman started to tell her to call and make an appointment for another day, but Virginia insisted it was important and that she'd wait until Dylan was available. She strode as confidently as she could to the benches and sat opposite the cross-legged man.

"What's this about?" Dylan was terse and unsmiling when she came to greet Virginia.

"Can we talk in your office?"

"I'm pretty busy. You didn't make an appointment." Dylan didn't answer the question, but Virginia started toward the hustle and bustle of the large open office space anyway and Dylan followed without objecting. "This way," she said, steering Virginia through a row of desks and toward a wall of small offices.

They entered Dylan's office, small and dark with no windows, and Virginia sat across the desk from Dylan and took in her surroundings. Pictures of Dylan with Marney over the years graced her desk, accompanied by unwashed coffee mugs and a scattered handful of peppermints. A filing cabinet occupied one corner of the room and a fake plant attempted to bring life to the space from another.

"What's this about?" Dylan repeated. She laced her fingers together and rested her chin on them, elbows on the desk.

"The Breeze Village murders."

Dylan sighed and shook her head at Virginia's response. "Look, I'm not working that case. I can set up a meeting between you and the lead detective on it if you'd like."

"Why aren't you on the case?" Virginia wanted to know.

"That's not the only case we're working on. We have lots of open cases and lots of superb officers and agents on every one of them. I happen not to be working that particular case."

Virginia shook her head. "I only want to talk to you about this." She reached across the desk and touched Dylan's hand with her own. When Dylan pulled away, it felt like a punch in the gut.

"You've got five minutes," Dylan said.

Virginia glanced up at the clock behind Dylan's head, nodded, and recounted her story of finding the pill bottles in Genie's cabinet.

Dylan nodded. "You told Detective Kincaid about those the night of the murders."

"Yes, but I'm not sure if he believed me or took me seriously. I wanted to make sure it got noted."

Dylan assured Virginia that it had been noted and started to stand, but Virginia continued. "I went back after the police left, and the pill bottles were gone. There wasn't an evidence tag like there were in the other places where police took items from the apartment."

"You snuck into a crime scene? That's off-limits."

"I think someone took the pills," Virginia pressed on. "Look, I saw Genie and Matt together in the parking lot the other day. And weeks ago, right around the time of Ruth's murder, I saw Genie sneaking around in the office at Breeze Village. The office connects to the nurses' station where they keep all the prescriptions."

"What were you doing there?"

"Someone took the pills from Genie's room," Virginia said, ignoring Dylan's question. "And they left a cup of tea behind."

This caught Dylan's attention. She asked Virginia how she knew the intruder left the tea behind, and Virginia told her about her visit with Genie and how Genie had mentioned her distaste for tea.

"She didn't have any in her room," Virginia said. "So whoever left it there brought it in themselves."

Dylan took notes on a small pad and thanked Virginia, but Virginia didn't stand to leave. "I think the tea was the murder weapon," she said instead.

"The lamp was the murder weapon," Dylan said simply.

"No, no, I mean it was intended to be the murder weapon, but Genie hated tea. So the murderer had to act fast and grab the lamp. But I think the murderer used the same method on Ruth, drugging her with a cup of tea."

"And Byron? How's he connected?"

Virginia shrugged and frowned. "In the wrong place at the wrong time?"

"That's an interesting theory, if a little far-fetched, but we already know Ruth wasn't poisoned."

Virginia shook her head. "Not with anything you'd think of as a poison. But with blood thinners. Ruth would never have taken too much of one of her prescriptions. She was too organized, too meticulous. But someone could have dissolved them in her tea and she would have taken them unsuspectingly."

Dylan looked Virginia in the eye and gave her a slightly sympathetic smile. "Even if that is what happened —and I'm not saying it is; it's still extremely far-fetched— that doesn't clue us in on who our killer is."

"It's Matt!" Virginia couldn't believe the words coming from Dylan's mouth. Matt had a connection to both Ruth and Genie and stood to gain from Ruth's death. And if he and Genie were involved in some shady drug-related business together, she had leverage on him, and leaving her alive was a risk. Virginia thought it was clear as day, but still, Dylan shook her head and dismissed her completely.

"Matt Beaumont is not a suspect in any of these deaths."

"How could he not be?" Virginia felt more confused than outraged. It didn't make sense.

"I can't tell you anything further." Dylan stood and walked around the desk to where Virginia sat, then extended a hand to help her up. "I'll pass what you've told me along to the appropriate officers."

Dylan led the way from her office, and Virginia followed silently. As they passed back through the bustling office space, Virginia asked Dylan to wait up. "Is there a restroom I could use?"

Inside the stall, Virginia was disappointed that the only thing the other officers occupying the restroom were interested in talking about was who wore what to a party the previous weekend. She had hoped to overhear some shop talk. Instead, she waited for them to leave the restroom, then slowly emerged, checking that Dylan had returned to her office. Rather than turning toward the exit, she began to navigate the cubicles, making her way toward a large conference room on the other side of the office space. Three large windows broke up the conference room wall, and through the open blinds, she could see a corkboard at the front of the room. In the center of the corkboard, as if at the head of the long conference table, was a picture of a Matt.

Virginia reeled from the sight. Not ten minutes ago, Dylan had insisted that Matt wasn't a suspect, and yet here was a picture of his face on a corkboard.

"Excuse me, ma'am, but you can't be here." An officer approached Virginia and whisked her away from the conference room. She emerged from the station and squinted into the afternoon sun. Why was Dylan so adamant Matt wasn't a suspect when he was clearly under investigation? Virginia glanced back at the station before heading to her car.

What are they hiding?

CHAPTER 21

The next morning Virginia drove to Breeze Village, unsure what she was after but knowing it was where she needed to be. She hadn't spoken to Marney in the four days since they discovered Genie and Byron. She wondered whether Marney had agreed to give therapy a try, whether she was traumatized thanks to Virginia involving her in the investigation.

The dining room was half full, and the scent of bacon and maple syrup filled the space. Virginia looked for Marney but didn't see her. She turned to leave, kicking herself for coming here, when she spotted Colleen sitting alone at a table in the corner.

"You seem troubled," Colleen said when Virginia approached.

"You had a vision about me?"

Colleen laughed. "No, dear. But I have eyes. Talk to me. What's the matter?" She patted the chair next to hers, and Virginia took it.

"Do you ever commune with earthly spirits?" Virginia

asked uncomfortably. "Like, the spirits of the living? Or is it just the departed?"

"What do you mean?"

"Well, you've talked about the spirit realm before, but I was wondering if maybe you could help me find someone? Someone alive?"

Colleen nodded slowly in understanding. "This is about your investigation."

Virginia thought Colleen would turn her away then and there, based on her reaction when Virginia had asked about Genie and Matt during their last meeting. Instead, Colleen turned to face Virginia and asked whether she had a photo, piece of clothing, or another personal item from the person she was looking for.

Virginia shook her head. "Would a drawing do?"

"Unfortunately not," Colleen said, turning back to her half-eaten plate of toast and eggs. As she stirred cream into her coffee, Virginia stood to leave her to finish her breakfast alone, when suddenly Colleen dropped her spoon to the table and stared off into the distance.

"Do you like tea?" she asked Virginia. "I'm getting a lot of energy around tea. That's odd." She seemed to snap out of whatever trance she'd been in and frowned at her cup of coffee, wondering aloud whether she'd picked the wrong beverage this morning.

"Actually," Virginia said, "I recently came into contact with a cup of tea I think is incredibly important." Her face flushed as she realized how silly she sounded, but Colleen nodded somberly as if that were a perfectly normal statement.

"In a styrofoam cup?"

Virginia nodded. "Can you sense the energy of anyone connected with the tea? Matt Beaumont, perhaps?" She hesitated before naming Matt, still worried Colleen would abruptly end the conversation, but Colleen didn't react. Instead, she shook her head and frowned slightly.

"I can't feel the specifics, but I'm getting a strong feminine energy. I'd say a woman brewed it. Granted, I generally find stronger connections with feminine spirits in the energetic plane, so I wouldn't rule anything out."

Virginia left Colleen, feeling frustrated. She was certain Matt was involved in the murders, and Colleen's comments about tea made her feel confident in her suspicion that the tea was the intended murder weapon, but she'd hoped Colleen could give her Matt's location. If the police kept insisting he wasn't a suspect, Virginia would surveil him herself, but first, she still needed to find him.

She started to cross the lobby and return to her car when she heard a familiar voice and turned to see Marney walking past, an enormous basket of yarn in her arms, and a small parade of elderly people following her.

"Marney!"

"What are you doing here?" Virginia worried Marney wouldn't want anything to do with her but was relieved to hear warmth in her voice. "I'm just about to teach a crochet class."

"Can I join you?" The words surprised her as they came out of her mouth. Virginia hadn't ever crocheted much, instead preferring to knit, and with her failing eyesight and arthritis, she'd put down the knitting needles years before. Still, she felt a warm comfort when Marney nodded enthusiastically and led her and the other excited class attendees into the activity room.

The room reminded Virginia of a grade school classroom. Long tables were pushed against the walls, and assorted wooden chairs formed a large circle with an opening at the front of the room. One chair sat in the opening, and Marney walked over to it and set the basket down beside it. The group that had followed her into the room took their seats in the circle and looked up at Marney expectantly. Virginia noticed Jane, the knitting woman she'd seen on the porch during her first visit to Breeze Village. She also recognized a few familiar faces from her poker game after Ruth's memorial.

Marney distributed materials and coached the class through crocheting dishcloths. Though different from the knitting projects she'd enjoyed before, Virginia found crocheting relaxing and familiar, and she was delighted to find that her new eyeglass prescription allowed her to see her work. Marney seemed to light up while teaching, walking around the room to help each person through the stitches, and Virginia felt proud to call Marney her oldest friend.

A few minutes into class, the door opened, and the class looked up to see Haley wheeling Midge into the room. "Sorry we're late," she said in a singsong voice, pushing Midge's wheelchair to join the circle. Before she could even get started on her project, Midge had a coughing fit and Haley hastily wheeled her back out of the room.

"Even in a retirement home, she can't get away from her kid," the woman next to Virginia joked. On the other side of her, a small man snorted with laughter.

"I've got three friends living with their kids right now on the waitlist for this place. Maybe the only way to get in is to have a kid on staff," another woman joked.

"I suppose that depends on how much your kid wants you here," the first woman chimed in. "If my daughter were a nurse here, she'd personally make sure I stayed on the waitlist as long as possible."

After the class, Virginia waited around, wonky dishcloth in hand, to talk with Marney. She helped Marney gather the materials back into her basket and walked with her to her cottage.

"How are you holding up?" she asked.

"I'm okay. Dylan wants me to go to therapy."

"Are you going to go?"

Marney shrugged. "I haven't decided yet. I think it's probably a good idea."

Virginia felt a pang of guilt. She tried to push the thought from her mind. "I talked with the police," she said.

"Dylan told me. Does that mean you'll step back and let them do their jobs?"

Virginia reeled a bit. "They've missed things before. I think they're still missing things." Marney opened her mouth to protest, but Virginia continued. "No one is giving this the attention it deserves. Just because it happened to old people in a retirement home doesn't mean homicide is suddenly no big deal!" Virginia's chest rose and fell, and she was surprised to find herself flushed and huffing. She hadn't intended to get so worked up.

"Listen," Marney said, shifting her basket to her hip and reaching out to put a hand on Virginia's arm, "I understand you need a win right now, to exercise your sense of agency amidst the changes taking place, but I really, really think you should leave this to the professionals."

Virginia narrowed her eyes and took a step back from Marney. "I need a win right now? Amidst the changes taking place? What are you talking about?"

Marney stammered, and Virginia's stomach dropped. She suddenly knew with certainty that Marney knew about Lawrence's impending move, had known Virginia was receiving offers from the same development company and had said nothing. She turned to walk away, biting her tongue between her teeth to hold back the tears until she was alone in her car.

"Virginia!" Marney called out behind her. "I'm sorry! I thought you'd talk to us when you were ready." But Marney didn't chase after her, and Virginia didn't turn around. The sting of betrayal ran deep, and she needed to get out of there.

* * *

A KNOCK on Virginia's door late the next morning tore her attention from the rerun of *NCIS Miami* she'd been watching as she sipped her coffee. She'd been unable to think about her investigation without remembering the betrayal by her closest friends, so she'd spent the previous afternoon and evening distracting herself with TV. Unfortunately, it had only been moderately effective; her

Marney held up one of the plastic grocery bags. "I brought Pub Subs." That was their name for the deli sandwiches from Publix, and Virginia's mouth watered at the mention of them. "And Oreos." Marney held up the other bag and laughed. "I wasn't sure how mad you'd be, so I came prepared. And there's one more thing."

Marney reached into her purse and pulled out a folded piece of lined paper. She handed it to Virginia, who warily unfolded it and found herself staring at an address. "It's Matt's," Marney said.

"How? Why?" Virginia gripped the back of a chair to steady herself. She'd been after this information for weeks, and now Marney, after insisting over and over again that she should drop the investigation, had handed it to her.

"I went to the station to bring Dylan a sandwich earlier—she's always eating microwaved crap for lunch—and did a little poking around. Just promise me you'll be careful. Even if Matt isn't the killer, I think you're right that he's involved somehow. At the very least, he's shady. I don't want you to get hurt."

Virginia nodded silently and carefully tucked the paper into her pocket as if it were a precious antique.

Not two hours later, just minutes after hugging Marney goodbye and watching her pull out of the driveway and turn the corner out of sight, Virginia climbed into her car, pulled out the slip of paper, and drove to Matt's house.

Matt's address was in a neighborhood not ten minutes from Virginia's house. She felt sick at the thought that she'd been so close to this man the whole time, and the closer she got, the faster her heart raced. Finally, she turned onto his street and slowed the car, counting the houses until she got to Matt's.

The small brick house had white doors and white aluminum awnings jutting out over the windows. Though the house itself was nothing special, the yard and garden were immaculate. Colorful blooms surrounded neatly trimmed bushes lining the front of the house, and Virginia admired the thought with which the garden had been laid out.

The honk of a car horn behind her startled Virginia, and she realized she'd nearly come to a complete stop in front of the house. She stepped on the gas and got moving, appeasing the driver behind her, and pulled out her phone.

"Gemma," she said into the receiver, "I think I've found another garden for the society to review."

CHAPTER 22

After the success of the Breeze Village feature in the *Review*, Gemma leapt at Virginia's suggestion. She'd suggested the group visit on Friday, but Virginia insisted the hyacinths were peaking and they needed to visit as soon as possible to get the best photos. Just two days later, the Garden Review Society eagerly descended on Matt's small brick house, cameras in hand.

A little tabby cat mewed and circled Virginia's legs as she surveyed the home. She peeked around the side of the house and saw a small shed with heavy-duty locks. As she approached the shed to peek into its tiny window, the front door squeaked open and a woman Virginia recognized from the family photo shown at Ruth's memorial poked her head out. She had long brown hair, a few gray hairs dotting the sleek braid that fell over her shoulder, and she wore an oversized t-shirt that hung off her slender frame.

"Can I help you?" she asked, voice harsh.

"Hi, we're here with the Seaview Garden Review Society," Gemma said. Her voice was sweet and she flashed a smile, but Virginia could tell the woman's unfriendly welcome surprised her.

"I did not authorize such a visit, and I won't participate. I'd appreciate it if you'd get off my property now, please."

Taken aback, Gemma stuttered and apologized. "Most people are excited to have their gardens featured. You've clearly worked hard on it, after all." She shot Virginia a wide-eyed look, and Virginia winced.

"Our last issue featured the gardens at Breeze Village," Virginia said. If they were going to be chased off the property, she at least wanted to make sure they got as much information as they could. She watched the woman's face for a reaction to the Breeze Village name, but her expression gave nothing away.

"Do you have any family there? Really lovely place," Virginia continued.

The woman stiffened a bit in the doorway. "No."

Virginia waited for her to elaborate, but she didn't.

"From your reaction, I'm guessing these gardens aren't your creations?"

"My husband's. Well, my mother-in-law before that, but he's the one who keeps them up now."

"They must be close." Virginia worked to keep a straight face, but her heart raced at the promise of extracting any fragment of information about Matt's relationship with his mother. She was surprised that he was so devoted to keeping up her gardens. There was not a weed in sight, and Virginia knew it was no small effort to keep them in this shape.

Matt's wife didn't answer Virginia.

Thinking on her feet, Virginia asked, "If gardening isn't your hobby, what is it you like to do?"

In her eighty years of life, Virginia had seldom met a person who didn't enjoy talking about themselves. As predicted, Matt's wife softened a bit, and a small smile even graced her face as she answered, "I'm a chef."

The smile didn't last. Virginia asked the woman what cuisine she cooked, and immediately a scowl took its place as the woman answered that here in Seaview people were only interested in heavy Southern food. "No one here has the palate to appreciate my work, but soon I'll be back where I'm appreciated." She nearly spat the words.

Before Virginia could ask where exactly "back where I'm appreciated" was, the woman looked around at the group of women taking pictures of the gardens and turned back to Virginia. "I think it's time for you to round up your friends and get off my property before I call the police."

Virginia didn't tell the woman she'd been trying to convince the police that this very house was a place of interest and that they should be surveilling it to see what Matt was up to. Instead, she turned to Gemma and apologized for not clearing the review with the residents first.

Gemma was clearly frustrated with Virginia. As the president of the society, she took it personally when a review went poorly, and she was the one who had to answer to the rest of the society members. Gemma herded the group back to their cars while Virginia tried to use these last precious moments to scope out the house. Other than the suspicious shed she'd noted earlier, there was nothing that caught her eye. The little gray tabby sat on the front steps and watched them gather their things to leave.

Matt's wife closed the door behind her when she was satisfied the group was on their way out. Virginia heard the lock turn behind her. She waved to Gemma as she pulled away, then began to climb into her own car when she saw a young man come out of the house two doors down. She glanced up at Matt's house to make sure his wife wasn't watching through the windows, then hurried over to the man and extended her hand to him.

"Can I help you?" The man took her hand gingerly, a confused look on his face. He looked from Virginia to his car parked on the curb and back, and Virginia knew she only had a minute before he excused himself to leave.

"I just moved in down the street and I saw an opportunity to meet a new neighbor, so I had to take it. I haven't met many people yet." She studied the man's face, but he wore the same impatient expression as before. "I just met the woman two houses down. Do you know her?"

The man perked up a bit. "Christine? Yeah, I've met her. A bit of a bitch, that one." Virginia recoiled at the language, but the man continued without seeming to notice. "She and her husband fight all the time. I guess that's why he spends all his time away from home. He's almost never around, and when he is, he's out in the garden. I keep telling them they need to bring their cat inside, that it's killing the local birds, but the wife won't hear it."

Virginia winced at the man's disdain for Christine but appreciated the insight. She thanked him and returned to her car as the man hurried to his own car and sped off. The last person in the world she wanted to feel sympathy for was Matt, but she couldn't help it after her encounter with Christine and her conversation with the neighbor. She sat in the driver's seat and recalled all her reasons for suspecting him, remembering his attitude when she'd run into him in Ruth's room during the memorial.

"He's the sketchy one," she whispered to herself. "He's not the victim here."

* * *

WHEN VIRGINIA PULLED up to her house ten minutes later, her stomach sank. There in the driveway waiting for her was pink suit-clad Chelsea. When Virginia stepped out of her car and started to make her way to the front door, Chelsea turned off her own car and stepped out. She waved a manicured hand at Virginia and smiled. Virginia scowled back.

"Why, hello, Virginia! I was beginning to wonder if you were ever coming home!" Chelsea's voice was saccharine, and Virginia felt rooted to the spot, suddenly unable to move. "I was wondering if you'd considered my offer any further?"

Rage bubbled up in Virginia. "You mean your offer to take my house out from under me for pennies compared to what it's worth? Yes, I considered it. No, I'm not interested."

"Interesting choice. It does make things a bit more difficult."

"I guess your luxury condos will just have to wait."

Virginia turned to continue toward the door, but Chelsea laughed behind her, causing her to turn around.

"Virginia," Chelsea spoke as if she were talking to a child, "we've bought up almost every house in the neighborhood. The ones we haven't bought yet? We're in negotiations on every one. I predict we'll be in the final stages within a week. The luxury condos are imminent."

"Well, you won't be in the final stages with *me* within a week." Virginia's answer felt weak coming from her mouth.

"Don't worry. If you are truly determined to hold out, we'll just build around you. I did say it makes things more difficult. We'll have to adjust the plans slightly. Later, when we do have your lot, we can put the pool and clubhouse there." Chelsea frowned slightly as she looked around her as if trying to envision the development. "Anyway, in the meantime, you'll just be surrounded on all sides by luxury condos. That is if you somehow manage to avoid the foreclosure, which I doubt. Then you can watch what being the lone old house surrounded by a luxury development does to your property values. I'll give you a hint: they won't be going up."

"Why are you doing this?"

Chelsea looked at Virginia, and Virginia thought she saw the tiniest hint of regret, or at least sympathy, flash in her eyes. But, if it was there, it vanished as quickly as it appeared. Chelsea cleared her throat and shrugged. "It's my job. Listen, Bellemeade is forward-thinking. We're bringing the future to Seaview. It's good for the town."

"Has it ever occurred to you that your fancy development isn't the future we want here in Seaview?"

"It has." Chelsea nodded. "That's why we did polls and market research and extensive studies before deciding that this is the site of Bellemeade's next venture." She cited similar condos that were flourishing in the other beach towns in the area, and Virginia's heart fell. Was she the only one who didn't want this for their town?

"You've got a week," Chelsea said, this time genuine kindness in her voice. "We'll even honor our first offer. I'll be back then to see what you decide. That's your last chance. After that, either you lose the house and Bellemeade scoops it up for cheap afterward, or you somehow manage to keep the house and you'll be living in the middle of a construction site in a matter of months."

When Chelsea was gone and Virginia was alone inside her house, she let her guard down and cried. Her body shook as she stumbled forward and gripped the back of the large recliner that separated the entryway from the living room. Her knuckles turned white as she dug her fingers into its plush upholstery, and she let herself cry until she was exhausted. Then, when the sounds of her own sobs quieted, the words Chelsea had left her with played over and over in her head. *You've got a week.*

On the long table in her dining room, Virginia could see the corner of the yellow paper sticking out from the pile of mail. It had been almost a month since she'd found it taped to her front door, and she still hadn't called the number it listed to set up a payment plan and straighten things out. Now, suddenly, she was faced with a deadline of a week to make a decision, and she knew she couldn't pretend any longer that she could handle the situation on her own.

Her eyes went to a framed picture on her mantle. In the photo, she, Lawrence, and Marney stood with their arms around each other and heads thrown back in laughter. They'd been at a Christmas party Lawrence's bowling league threw years before, and in that moment, they looked so carefree. In that moment, they *were* so carefree.

When Earl died, Lawrence and Marney were the ones who arranged the funeral. They took care of every detail, just giving Virginia instructions on where to be and when. They'd held her hand, brought her meals, cleaned her house. Marney had even held her up in the shower and shampooed her tangled hair when the grief brought her to her knees and she thought she couldn't go on.

Marney and Lawrence had been there for Virginia when she needed help before, not waiting for her to ask. They knew her, and they knew she'd never ask. But this time, they didn't know what she was facing, so they couldn't jump in and help on their own. Virginia was going to need to ask for help.

She glanced out the window toward Lawrence's house. She hadn't spoken to him since their fight, when she'd learned he was selling his house to the developers and moving to some seaside condo. She decided she'd start with Marney.

CHAPTER 23

Virginia drove past Breeze Village three times before parking, then sat in her car to collect herself before going inside. Her stomach was in knots and her face was still puffy and red from the afternoon spent crying. Part of her wished Marney would be gone for the evening, out on some date, so Virginia could knock on her door and then go home and still say she'd tried, but she knew that wouldn't be the case. She pushed the image of Byron's body from her mind.

Dusk was falling over Seaview, and the moss hanging from the old oak trees swayed in the evening breeze. A nearly full moon provided ample light and threw shadows over the mostly empty parking lot. Virginia looked up at the moon and inhaled, trying to center herself, imagining she could form a connection and pull energy and strength from the moon. Stephanie had led her in a full moon ritual years before, and Virginia tried to recapture that energy. She had to stifle a giggle at the ridiculousness, but as she took her first steps toward the main building, she felt more confident than she had before. Though she still hated the idea of confessing to her friends the situation she'd gotten herself into, she knew deep down that she couldn't keep trying to get out of it on her own.

Before she gripped the door handle, Virginia breathed in to a count of four and out to a count of eight, then pushed the door open. Her newfound calm was immediately dispelled as she found herself face-to-face with Marney immediately. She threw her hand to her chest, startled, and Marney gave her an inquisitive look.

"What's going on?" Worry drenched her voice.

"I came to talk to you." Virginia realized for the first time that Marney was carrying her crochet basket. "Is there another class tonight? It seems awfully late."

Marney shook her head and explained that she'd been crocheting with some of the ladies earlier and Jane had left a book behind. "I'm taking it to her now, but then I'll be heading back to my cottage. Do you want to go wait for me there?"

The concern in her voice reminded Virginia of her blotchy appearance, and she quickly shook her head no. "I'll go with you."

The two stepped into the elevator together and tension filled the small space. Virginia hadn't seen Marney since she'd gotten Matt's address from the police station, but she had a feeling now wasn't the time to bring up the investigation.

"What did you come to talk to me about?"

Marney's words surprised Virginia. She'd hoped the conversation could wait until they were alone in Marney's cottage. The elevator dinged, and they stepped out onto the third floor, starting down the hall in the opposite direction of Colleen's room. Though the hallway was deserted and all the doors were closed, Virginia felt the words stick in the back of her throat. She couldn't talk about it here.

"No one's around. Virginia, what's going on?" Concern dripped from Marney's voice, and Virginia sighed.

"You already know about the developer coming around Grove Park, but there's more to it than that. It's why I've been working at the doctor's office."

Before Virginia could say any more, Haley rounded the corner at the end of the hallway, walking toward them. She gave them a slight smile before turning to a door on her right, opening it, and stepping inside. In her hand, she held a styrofoam cup. Virginia froze, not hearing Marney's concerned questions.

Instead, in her head, Virginia heard Colleen's words. *I'm getting a strong feminine energy. I'd say it was brewed by a woman.* Haley had been first on the scene at both Ruth's death and Genie's and Byron's murders. *Maybe the only way to get in is to have a kid on staff... I suppose that depends on how much your kid wants you there.* The conversation Virginia had overheard during Marney's crochet class joined Colleen's words, swirling in Virginia's mind like a chaotic symphony. Haley's mom had only gotten off the waitlist because Ruth was murdered. How badly had Haley wanted to secure a spot for her mom?

"Whose room is that?"

"Ronald's." Marney was still watching Virginia with a concerned look, but Virginia was oblivious. Unthinking, without realizing what she was doing, Virginia moved toward the door.

"Stop!" she shouted. When she threw the door open, Virginia saw Haley's and Ronald's shocked faces. Ronald lowered a cup of tea from his lips, and Virginia yelled, "Don't drink that. It's drugged!" She crossed the room and knocked the cup out of Ronald's hand.

"What are you doing?" Marney rushed into the room to find Ronald screaming in pain, hot tea burning his lap while the styrofoam cup lay on its side on the floor. Haley grabbed both of Virginia's arms, holding them behind Virginia's back and tugging her backward away from Ronald. Her grip was so firm Virginia knew she would have bruises the next day.

"Get off me, you murderer!"

Haley radioed for assistance, and within minutes, the room was swarming with staff. Virginia was dragged from the room while nurses tended to Ronald's burns. Marney looked on in horror as Virginia shouted accusations at Haley. Her face was flushed and spit flew from her lips. "You killed them! How could you?"

Marney tried to calm Virginia down, but Virginia was inconsolable, insisting Haley not be let out of sight. Only when she was assured Haley wasn't going anywhere could Virginia begin to focus her eyes on Marney and register her fear. Slowly, she realized Marney's fear wasn't of Haley; it was of Virginia. The realization cut like a knife, and tears began to flow down her still-swollen cheeks. She wondered how she had any left.

"Mrs. Walker."

Virginia wiped the tears from her eyes with the backs

eating pudding with her mother in blood-stained clothes as if it were nothing. As if she hadn't bludgeoned two people to death hours before.

"You know exactly what you've done. You killed Ruth. You drugged her tea to make it look like an accidental overdose on prescription medication. Then, when you tried to do the same to Genie, you were surprised to learn she hates tea. Your plan was foiled; a struggle ensued. Byron was in the wrong place at the wrong time. And now here you were, about to do the same thing to Ronald!"

Haley's thin lips formed a frown, and her eyes began to water. "You think I killed them? Residents I looked after for years? Who I loved?"

Virginia wanted to yell at her. She wanted Dylan to yell at her, to tell her the waterworks weren't going to help her now. Instead, Dylan wrapped a sympathetic arm around Haley's shoulders.

"Haley didn't kill anyone," Dylan said, turning to Virginia. The disapproval in her voice stung.

"Why would I do that?" Haley continued. "My whole life is dedicated to caring for the residents here."

"Your mother was on the waitlist. Everyone is talking about it, about what you'd be willing to do to get her off the waitlist and into a room. She even said you're the only reason she's here."

Haley wiped a tear from her eye, and black eyeliner smeared on her hand. "I knew everyone talked about me behind my back. I didn't know anyone thought I was capable of murder."

Haley looked down at her feet, wiping more tears

from her cheeks, then looked up at Virginia with furrowed brows. "If my whole motive was to get my mom into Breeze Village, why would I have tried to kill Genie or Ronald? She moved into Ruth's room."

"I, err," Virginia stammered, not sure how to respond.

"No," Haley said, her voice growing louder and more confident. "I didn't kill Ruth. I didn't kill anyone. I didn't drug Ronald's tea. And I'm tired of people gossiping about me as if I'm a horrible person just because my mom moved in here." She turned to Dylan. "If you or any of your officers have questions for me, I'll be happy to answer them, but I'm not humoring this one any longer." She shot Virginia a glare as she spat the words "this one," then turned and walked away to join the nurses attending to Ronald.

"I don't think it'll come as a surprise, but you won't be allowed back on Breeze Village property," Michelle piped up.

Virginia inhaled sharply. It did come as a surprise. Virginia was the only one taking the murders seriously and looking out for Breeze Village residents, and now she was banned from the premises?

"I'll reach out to you if we have further questions." Dylan waited expectantly, and Virginia rose and started toward the elevator. Marney looked on with sad eyes, and the look on her face made Virginia's face flush with embarrassment. It was pity.

Virginia kept her head down as she entered the elevator. She was relieved when the chime sounded and she stepped out to find the main floor empty. The cool night air felt soothing on her skin, swollen and sensitive from the day's tears, and she walked in a daze to her car.

Halfway home, the rain began to fall, and it didn't let up. Honking horns joined the chorus of disapproval playing in Virginia's head, the words from Haley and Dylan swirling over and over through her mind. She pulled off to the side to let others pass, driving at a crawl through the blinding rain.

When she finally arrived home nearly an hour later, Virginia flipped the light switch in the entryway and was surprised when no light filled the space. She moved into the living room, shuffling her feet across the floor to avoid tripping over any unseen objects, and tried switching on the lamp. Nothing.

As her eyes adjusted to the dark, Virginia noticed a piece of paper on the floor. She picked it up, groaning as she bent her stiff body toward the floor, and her heart sank when she realized what it was. In her hand, she held a blue sticky note written in her handwriting: *electric bill due.*

CHAPTER 24

"Where have you been?" Dr. DiMarco stood behind the reception desk, folders in his hands and a harried look on his face. "It's after ten!"

After a cold shower the night before, Virginia had fallen into a deep sleep and remained that way until the sun peeking in through her curtains woke her. Her alarm clock's battery backup was dead, and without electricity, she hadn't been able to charge her phone, so she couldn't call to alert the doctor that she was running late.

The waiting room was full, and Virginia hurried to the desk to take over so Dr. DiMarco could lead the next patient back to the exam room. The next hour passed in the blink of an eye, a blur of phone calls and walk-ins that took Virginia from flustered to entirely off-balance. Amidst the swirl of demands, she mixed up a set of lab results, pulling the wrong file for a long-time patient, and Dr. DiMarco came storming out of the exam room toward her desk.

Virginia felt the eyes of the waiting patients turn to

her as the doctor approached her desk and asked in a hiss if he could speak to her privately. In an empty exam room, he threw down the folder in his hand and gestured to it. "What is this?"

Tears welled up in Virginia's eyes as he berated her for making a mistake, listing off the potential consequences of mixing up patient files and lab results.

"I could have told this healthy man he had cancer! I could have told a cancer patient he was cancer-free! I could have given someone the wrong procedure. Do you understand how serious this could have been?"

Virginia could barely bring herself to nod.

"Just go home. I'll handle things here myself." Disgust and disappointment dripped from the doctor's words.

Virginia's head spun. She wasn't sure if she was being fired or just dismissed for the day. Either way, she couldn't afford the loss.

When the doctor saw her expression, his face softened slightly. "I went through this with my mom. It might be time to look into other arrangements. I know how much it means to you to have work, to have something to do, but I think you should think about what's really best. We moved my mom into Breeze Village. She was reluctant at first, but we had a wonderful experience with them. You should look into it."

Virginia turned and left the exam room without answering. She knew that if she tried, her voice would fail her. She picked up her purse from the back of her chair and left the office, feeling the stares from the waiting room following her.

Outside, in her car, Virginia sat behind the wheel

wondering where to go from here. She couldn't visit Marney in Breeze Village, her home was a dark reminder of her failure to look after herself, and she was sure Lawrence had heard about the previous night's incident, so she also ruled out talking to him. As she flipped through her options in her mind, rejecting each in turn, she felt her heart rate speeding up and her breathing becoming shallow. She was out of options and overwhelmed.

With no place else to go, Virginia drove to the beach and walked along the shoreline. The sky was a brilliant blue and the sun warmed the air. A gentle breeze blew, and a few white, fluffy clouds sat above the horizon. It was an absolutely gorgeous morning. Virginia was disgusted. As she walked, her toes digging into the cool sand, she wished for dark storm clouds to roll in and for torrential rain to pummel the surrounding beach. She wanted thunder and lightning, a squall to chase away the giggling tourists. She wanted the universe to show itself for the relentless and destructive place she knew it was.

Her mind swirling with dark thoughts, Virginia bought a cup of french fries from a portly vendor with a blue and yellow cart and continued her walk, alternating munching on the salty fries and throwing them for the seagulls. More birds swarmed, calling out for food, and she welcomed the chaos. After tossing the last of her fries for the birds to enjoy, Virginia sat on a wooden swing and rocked herself, looking out at the families and couples occupying the sand between her and the waves. She wondered if it were spring break and wished the beachgoers had chosen any other spot for their getaways.

Nearest to her was a young couple, tanned and trim, tossing a frisbee back and forth and periodically running over to their setup to stop their towels from blowing away in the breeze. Virginia wondered what lay ahead for them, if the young girl would find herself a widow sooner than she'd ever imagined, raising two children on her own. She watched them play, pity in her heart for the hardships she knew life would throw at them. She felt swallowed up by envy that they hadn't yet known those hardships.

Further down the beach was a couple with two children: a little girl with blond ringlets and a frilly pink swimsuit, and a bald little baby wearing a sunhat to protect his head. The couple argued as they worked together to set up a small tent and umbrella. Virginia imagined them divorcing before the little girl turned five, a bitter custody battle ensuing. Those kids would toss their parents into nursing homes at the first opportunity, she thought.

As Virginia sat stewing in her dark daydreams, a small green soccer ball rolled toward her, tapping her foot. She looked up to see another young family to her left, three small boys running around and arguing about the bounds of their soccer field. The youngest of the three, small with dark skin and curly hair, ran up to her and grabbed the ball. Before he returned to his brothers, he looked up at Virginia and smiled at her, a big snaggle-toothed grin full of optimism, and as he ran off back to his family, she felt the tears start to flow.

* * *

THE NEXT MORNING, Virginia arrived at work early, two coffees in hand. After leaving the beach the day before, she'd gone to the store to get a battery-powered alarm clock, and after another cold shower that morning she'd driven through the McDonald's drive-thru and picked up breakfast and coffee for herself and Dr. DiMarco. She wasn't sure whether she still had a job that morning, but she figured bringing a gesture of goodwill couldn't hurt her chances.

"Good morning." Dr. DiMarco was sitting behind the reception desk looking at the computer and turned and raised an eyebrow at Virginia when she entered the office. "I brought you a coffee." She held the cup up and then set it on the counter in front of him.

The doctor didn't respond but picked up the cup and took a sip, nodding appreciatively before setting it back down.

Virginia peered over her boss's shoulder and saw him struggling to reschedule an appointment. One of the less intuitive interfaces in their scheduling software was stumping him, and before she realized what she was doing, she was showing him how to work it. When she'd finished scheduling the appointment, he looked up at her and her face flushed. She wasn't even sure if he'd expected her back or whether she still worked there, and she worried she was overstepping.

"I'm sorry," he said before she could say anything. "And thank you." He nodded to the cup of coffee and gave Virginia a small smile before standing up and gesturing to the chair. "All yours."

Before he could leave the waiting room, Virginia

called out, "Wait!" He turned to look at her, and she swallowed and cleared her throat before continuing. "While I'm not looking for any more unsolicited advice on whether I should continue living on my own, there is something I could use your help with." She worried she was too harsh, but though she knew she had messed up, she still hadn't completely forgiven him for his assumptions and unsolicited advice the day before.

"What can I help you with?"

Relieved that he didn't seem upset, she continued, her voice coming out soft and hesitant. "I know there are places that specialize in helping, err, people of a certain age with technology. Could you help me find the phone number for one? I'd like to see if they can help me."

"Of course." Without saying anything more or making a big deal out of it, Dr. DiMarco pulled his phone from his pocket and searched for a local resource center. He read off a phone number for Virginia to write on one of her sticky notes, then turned and headed into one of the exam rooms without another word.

Okay. Virginia looked down at the seven digits scrawled on her blue notepad. *Maybe I do forgive him.*

If asking for the number was difficult, bringing herself to dial it once she was back in the comfort of her home was like trying to convince herself to cut off her own finger. What were they going to say to her? Would they be nice? What if the person recognized her voice and told someone she'd called and asked for help? Virginia practiced a deep breathing exercise she'd seen Stephanie teach Marney to help manage her panic attacks, then counted to three and dialed the number before she had a chance to think any more about it.

It rang three times before anyone answered, and Virginia had just pulled the phone away from her face to hang up when she heard a young woman's voice say, "Hello, Seaview area Elder Resource Center. This is Kayla speaking. How can I help you today?"

"Err, hi, Kayla. My name is Virginia Walker. I was wondering if you knew how I can use my phone to set up reminders for things? I've seen my kids do it before and I think I ought to give it a try."

Virginia waited for the woman to laugh or make fun of her, but she didn't. Instead, in a cheery voice, she responded, "Of course! Do you know what kind of phone you have?"

Kayla talked Virginia through putting the call on speakerphone so she could navigate away from the call screen and set up reminders for trash day and morning and evening medications. She was so patient and kind that Virginia found herself feeling at ease, the embarrassment around asking for help fading away.

"I'm going to go see if I can find my bill due dates so I can put those in here, too," Virginia said, her confidence growing.

"Ma'am, are you familiar with auto-pay?"

"Oh, no, I don't have a car loan. I paid that off years ago."

A giggle came through the phone line and Virginia wondered what she'd said to make the woman on the other end laugh. "Not 'auto' as in car. 'Auto' as in 'automatic.' You can set up most bills these days to automatically withdraw from a bank account so you don't have to remember to pay it. You'd just need to make sure you keep enough in your account to cover your bills."

Virginia's jaw dropped. It felt like someone had just handed her a lifeline. The money was still a concern, of course, but as long as she avoided making any more serious mistakes at work, she shouldn't be in too much danger there. Now she wouldn't ever have to stick another note to the wall reminding her of an upcoming due date.

"How can I set that up?"

Kayla began walking Virginia through the steps, but when she reached into her purse, Virginia couldn't find her checkbook. She checked the kitchen counter, bedside table, and rifled through the piles of mail on the buffet table in the dining room, but came up empty.

Unfazed, Kayla said, "Let me just walk you through what you'll need to do when you find your account information so you'll be all set when you have that."

Virginia closed her eyes and looked up at the ceiling, thanking the heavens for sending an angel in the form of this elder resource center worker.

When Kayla asked, "Is there anything else I can help you with today?" Virginia wanted to say no and hang up the phone. Instead, she took a deep breath and asked whether the resource center also had a legal aid department.

"I recently found out about a tax lien on my house, and I'm just not sure what to make of the situation or how to rectify it. I could use some help." The words falling from her lips surprised Virginia, but Kayla again seemed entirely unfazed. She said cheerfully that they did offer legal aid and then transferred Virginia.

Virginia tapped her foot lightly as she listened to the ringing tone and waited for someone to pick up. Her pulse had slowed, and she found herself feeling almost relaxed. She was still uncomfortable asking for help, but for the first time, it felt like there was hope.

"Hello?" a man answered the phone, his voice gruff.

"Hi, is this the legal aid department of the resource center?"

"Yes." He didn't say anything further, and Virginia recoiled at the contrast to Kayla's welcoming tone just moments before.

"Erm, I had a letter posted to my door a few weeks ago letting me know my house was being foreclosed due to missed property tax payments. I was hoping to have someone help walk me through the timeline and how I might be able to set up a payment plan or what I can do to stop that from happening?"

The man on the other end of the line paused, and the silence filled Virginia with worry. When he finally responded, he asked Virginia about the letter she'd received, and she stammered, trying to find it in the pile of papers on her table. While she rifled through the stack, the man grumbled that she needed his help but hadn't had the decency to come prepared. Overwhelmed, Virginia hung up before he could say more and before she had the chance to read him the letter so he could help her decipher the meaning behind the legalese.

In less than a minute, she'd gone from feeling glad she'd asked for help, feeling the first bit of hope she'd felt in a long time, to regretting picking up the phone in the first place.

Her phone chimed, and Virginia looked down to see a reminder to put her trash out that evening, one of the reminders she'd set up with Kayla's help just minutes before. Her stomach dropped and she immediately felt resentment bubble up inside her, frustration that she couldn't remember the necessary little details herself. She was angry that she'd have forgotten entirely had her phone not reminded her, and angry that she'd needed help to get the phone to remind her. The one positive was that she wouldn't look out the window to see Lawrence wheeling the bin down to the curb himself when he noticed she'd forgotten.

CHAPTER 25

The morning sun streamed through the gauzy curtains and into Virginia's dining room the next day as she gathered up bills and documents to take to the bank. She planned to order a new checkbook and ask about setting up auto-pay for some of her bills, and she'd spent the last hour sipping coffee and sorting mail. Months of unopened bills and letters were now sorted into neat stacks, and though it had been an overwhelming task, a new calmness came over Virginia now that it was nearly complete.

Toward the bottom of the pile, a flier with pictures of flowers on it caught her eye, and Virginia picked it up to find that it was a flier for an artisan's market and festival the town was putting on. She checked the date and realized with a sinking feeling that it was that very day, and Marney was going to be there selling her crocheted goods and teaching a short beginner's class. The Breeze Village crochet club had urged Marney to show off her goods and teach a class there after her classes at Breeze Village had

of the park, overflowing with local makers showing off their goods, and carnival rides and food trucks dotted the lawn. Families laid out picnic blankets, friends tossed frisbees and kicked soccer balls back and forth, and a small stage featured a live band. It wasn't even noon yet, but the energy was high. Virginia felt her mood lift by a degree just stepping into that atmosphere, though nerves at seeing Marney for the first time since the incident with Haley and Ronald fluttered in her stomach.

As she walked around the park searching for Marney, Virginia passed vendors selling clothes, bags, hand-bound notebooks and journals, beautifully detailed embroidery, jewelry, candles, and more. Each booth caught her eye, and she thought that once she'd found Marney, she'd like to come back to visit the rest of the vendors. She could knock out her Christmas shopping before Easter!

Virginia tore her gaze away from a vendor selling shimmering wind chimes, and then, after walking nearly half the perimeter of the park, she spied Marney two tables away. Marney's display comprised a small table covered with a white tablecloth positively covered in crocheted goods. Hats, socks, and scarves took up most of the table, with blankets stacked on the end. Though Marney could turn yarn into some of the most beautiful creations Virginia had laid eyes on, she clearly didn't have a knack for displaying her goods, and Virginia's heart ached as she saw Marney looking longingly at the patrons walking past her table without stopping.

"Marney!" Virginia called, waving to her friend as she approached the table. Relief flooded Virginia when Marney saw her and lit up with a genuine smile and wave.

When Virginia reached Marney's display, Marney wrapped her in a tight hug and Virginia bit her tongue to hold back tears. She'd been so nervous about how she would be received, and to be met with love felt like grace she didn't think she deserved.

"I brought you some flowers," she said. "For your display."

The two of them rearranged the display table, and when Virginia stepped back to take it in she broke into a grin. It looked wonderful. Immediately, a group of three women approached the table and started asking Marney about her prices, fingering the soft blankets and shawls with appreciation. They each bought at least one item, and Virginia squeezed Marney's arm and flashed her a smile as they walked away.

"Thank you for coming," Marney said, her voice soft. "And for helping with the display. You know I'm dreadful at that sort of thing."

"Why isn't Lawrence here helping, too?" Virginia wanted to know.

"He's got a bowling match. I felt bad not being able to make it to watch them. They're up against their rivals from Beachwood this week."

Virginia hadn't even remembered Lawrence had a bowling match that day, much less who they were facing, and the realization of how much she relied on Marney and Lawrence to each help her remember what the other had going on in their life surprised her. She'd never make it to Lawerence's games without Marney inviting her and picking her up to take her, and she'd never remember Marney's events if Lawrence didn't remind her.

"How did your class go?" Virginia asked, hoping to take her mind off her failings as a friend, but at the mention of the class, Marney's face fell.

"Only three people showed up."

"Oh, honey." Virginia wrapped Marney in a hug. "I bet those three people had fun, though, right? I'm so sorry I wasn't here."

Marney assured her it was fine, that those three people did have a great time, that she had just gotten her hopes up a little too much, but Virginia could hear the disappointment in her voice.

Another group approached, and Virginia stood back while Marney talked with them about the yarns she'd used for different projects and how she'd gotten started crocheting decades before. The group walked away, arms laden with blankets, and Marney counted out the bills they'd handed her before stuffing it in her cash box and giving Virginia a triumphant smile and a thumbs up.

"I have something else to tell you," Marney said, looking around and then leaning in close. Virginia's curiosity was piqued, and she leaned in expectantly. "There was a break-in at Breeze Village this week, on Tuesday." That was the same night Virginia had burst in on Haley and been banned from the premises.

Eyes wide, Virginia tried to process what Marney was telling her. "While the cops were there?"

Marney shrugged. "I don't know when during the night. No one realized anything was amiss until Wednesday morning."

"What did they take?"

Marney looked around them again before whispering, "Painkillers."

Virginia's jaw dropped as Marney told her how someone had broken into the main office and stolen prescription painkillers from the nurses' station. The memory of meeting Genie in the office at night immediately flashed in Virginia's mind.

"Get this," Marney continued. "When they were taking inventory of what had been stolen, they went through the records and found a bunch of prescriptions none of the staff had any recollection of. Someone had been forging prescriptions and then stealing them before they could be distributed to the residents."

"Genie," Virginia said confidently. "It had to have been her. The pill bottles in her room, and the night I saw her in the office acting suspicious..."

Marney nodded. "But Genie's dead, so who stole the drugs this week?"

"Matt." Virginia didn't hesitate before answering, and to her surprise, Marney didn't immediately push back. Virginia hadn't realized how much she needed someone to validate her, nod their head, and not immediately dismiss her theory.

"It makes the most sense," Marney agreed, "but if he and Genie were in this together, why would he murder his partner?"

"To keep her from talking, maybe." Before Virginia could consider this any further, her phone chimed, and she looked down at it to see a reminder that she had a shift at the doctor's office that afternoon. "I learned how to put my calendar in here," she said proudly, holding her phone up for Marney to see. "I've got to go to work."

"What time do you get off? Can we have dinner together later?" For the first time since Ruth's death, Marney seemed curious about the case and eager to discuss it with Virginia, and as Virginia bid her friend adieu, she had a spring in her step.

* * *

Before Virginia rounded the corner, a familiar voice behind her made her turn, and she saw Dylan standing in front of Marney's booth, gesturing to the display and cooing over her mother's hard work. Virginia crept closer, wondering if Marney would ask Dylan about the break-in.

Instead, when she got within earshot, she was disappointed to hear that their conversation was entirely centered around what Dylan's office neighbor had brought for lunch that day. Marney giggled as Dylan described the smell of his unrefrigerated tuna salad filling the break room.

"Ma'am, can I help you?" Virginia jumped and turned to see the vendor for the display she'd been staring at absentmindedly looking at her expectantly. She shook her head and apologized, then turned to leave, but just as she started to walk away, she heard the sound of Dylan's radio.

"Eyes on the suspect," a voice said, partially obscured by static.

Dylan excused herself and stepped off the sidewalk

toward a cluster of trees where she pulled out her cell phone, and Virginia crossed the sidewalk to stand on the other side of a display of handmade drums from where Dylan stood. The vendor asked if Virginia was looking for anything in particular. She assured him she was just browsing and didn't need any help, willing him to walk away and leave her to listen in on Dylan's conversation.

"Confirmed eyes on Beaumont?" Virginia heard Dylan ask. Her heartbeat thumped in her ear, the excitement rising in her chest. "Maintain eyes but do not move in." Though she strained to listen, Virginia couldn't make out the rest of Dylan's conversation, but before Dylan hung up, Virginia was certain she heard Dylan say "Clairmont and Seventh," an intersection she knew was across town in an industrial area of Seaview.

As Dylan returned to Marney's display, Virginia ducked her head and resumed trying to look interested in a pair of bongos. Behind her, she heard Dylan apologize for the short visit and Marney insist that it was fine. Virginia counted to thirty, thinking that by then Dylan would be out of the area, then hurried back over to where Marney stood straightening her crocheted items on the table in front of her.

"Virginia, you're back," Marney said, surprised.

"Did you hear any of Dylan's conversation just now?"

Marney frowned and shook her head. "I thought you had gone. You were listening in?"

"I was on my way out when I heard Dylan's voice, then I heard her radio go off and someone mention tailing some suspect. Marney, the suspect is Matt!" Virginia couldn't contain her excitement. She'd been right all along, and now the police were finally closing in on the killer.

Marney looked stunned. "Are you sure?"

"They said Beaumont," Virginia said, nodding. "And I heard the location. We have to go see what's going on!"

"Whoa," Marney said, throwing up her hands in front of her and stepping backward. She shook her head. "We cannot go crash a police stakeout. And besides, you have work."

Virginia hesitated. In the few minutes since her phone had reminded her of her upcoming shift at work, she'd entirely forgotten about it. She felt torn, knowing she was on thin ice at work and that if she didn't leave now, she'd be late. Under the noon sun, with crowds bustling around her, Virginia weighed her options.

She could either go to work and risk letting a killer go free, trusting that the police would take him down, or she could go after Matt, taking justice into her own hands, but risk losing her job. The past conversations Virginia had had with the police played in her head: Officer Matthews dismissing her completely, Detective Kincaid perking up at the mention of Matt's name, and Dylan insisting Matt wasn't a suspect when he clearly was. In that moment, she knew she had to go after Matt.

Whether or not she kept her job, Virginia decided saving her house was a losing battle. One way or another, Bellemeade was going to win that fight. But she could still get justice for Ruth, Genie, and Byron.

"I can't leave this in the hands of the police," Virginia said, looking at Marney with pleading eyes. "Not after everything they've overlooked and dismissed on this case."

Marney protested, but Virginia held firm. "I'm going to go either way. Are you going to come with me?"

With a sigh, Marney agreed. "The rules are," she said as they abandoned the table, arms laden with crocheted goods as they hurried to Virginia's car, "we stay low. We are observing only. Nothing more."

Virginia nodded, willing to agree to anything to get Marney in the car with her, and sped off across town to take down a murderer.

CHAPTER 26

The southern outskirts of Seaview consisted mainly of a series of warehouses and industrial parks. Traffic thinned as Virginia and Marney made their way down Seventh Street, leaving downtown first, then the residential ring around it, and finally entering the business district.

Virginia strained her neck, trying to read the street signs they passed, looking for Clairmont. As she squinted at an approaching sign, trying to make out the letters, Marney sat up beside her and gasped. "Look, there he is!" Marney pointed out her window, and Virginia turned to see Matt walking along the sidewalk toward them, a large black duffel bag in hand. He was nearly two blocks away but walking quickly, and Virginia nearly pulled the car up onto the sidewalk, completely distracted and unable to take her eyes off him.

"Keep going. We don't want him to see us," Marney hissed.

"I don't want to lose him," Virginia hissed back. The

two continued their whispered argument as if Matt would hear them if they spoke at a normal volume.

"The police are nearby. They said they had eyes on him, right? So they're hiding somewhere in the vicinity. We said we were just going to observe."

Virginia pulled over and parked among the empty vans and cars that lined the road. She looked around for any sign of the police but saw nothing. Though she knew they were likely to be crouched in some unmarked van, she couldn't help but worry they weren't actually there at all.

"Here he comes. Lay your seat down so he won't see you," Marney instructed.

"I can't. My back will seize up." Virginia gestured to the ergonomic pillow she'd attached to her seat back.

As Marney protested, Virginia's eyes widened, and she said, "Get down, get down."

Marney pulled the lever to recline her seat as far as it would go, and Virginia hunched over as much as she could with her seat in its upright position. Despite their efforts, as Matt walked by, he turned his head and looked directly into their car window. His eyes met Virginia's, and for a moment she thought he'd pull out a gun then and there. Instead, he kept walking.

"He saw us," Virginia said, her heart pounding in her chest.

"What?" Marney sat up, looking from Virginia's pale face to Matt's back as he continued down the sidewalk as if nothing were amiss. "Are you sure?"

"Positive."

Virginia followed Matt with her eyes, scanning the

warehouses and buildings he passed, trying to figure out where he was headed. She inhaled sharply when she saw a warehouse to his right with three cars running right outside. "That has to be it," she breathed, pointing.

Marney nodded, and the two watched with bated breath as he approached the warehouse, then kept walking straight past. "What's he doing?"

"It's got to be because he saw us," Virginia said. She cursed and kept her eyes on Matt. The cars in front of the warehouse hadn't moved. Did they know something was up? Virginia's stomach sank as she thought about how long she'd tried to track down Matt, to find something the police could bring him in for, and now in her overzealous attempt to bring him down herself, she might have blown a police operation and caused a killer to go free.

Not today. She gripped the door handle and stepped out of the car.

Marney panicked and reached out to grab her arm. "What are you doing?" she hissed.

"He's bailing," Virginia said. "Because of us, he's not going through with whatever was about to go down. I can't let him get away."

Without waiting for Marney's response, Virginia straightened up and raised her voice. "Hey, Matt," she yelled.

He stiffened but kept walking, and she began to hobble behind him, moving as quickly as she could but cursing her stiff legs.

"What's in the bag?"

This time, Matt paused and turned to face Virginia.

Almost a block separated them, and Virginia continued toward him while he stood still.

"Stolen painkillers?"

"Back off." Matt's voice was scratchy as if he'd been crying.

Virginia was surprised. It wasn't the same self-assured voice he'd used when he'd threatened her in Ruth's room during the memorial. He turned back around and resumed walking, but Virginia persisted. Behind her, she heard the passenger side door open and close as Marney stepped out to follow her.

"Why'd you do it? Kill your own mom and then your business partner? We figured it out, you know."

"Whatever you think you know, you're wrong." Matt whipped around, reaching to his side and then pointing a small pistol straight at Virginia.

The breath caught in her throat, and she couldn't have spoken if she'd tried.

"That's right," Matt said. "Just shut up and go back to your car." He kept his gun trained on Virginia and she stood stock straight, unable to will her legs to move.

Behind her, Virginia heard a thud and saw Matt's eyes widen in surprise. When she turned, she saw Marney lying on the concrete, unconscious. Her eyes moved from Marney to Matt, and he tossed his gun and the duffel bag off to the side of the road before taking off at a run. The three cars that had been running in front of the warehouse peeled out, one after the other, and sped away.

All at once, the back doors of a van across the street swung open and Dylan jumped out, accompanied by two other officers. Dylan ran toward where Virginia stood over Marney, yelling, "Mom!" The other two officers took off at a sprint toward Matt. Sirens sounded somewhere nearby.

"What did you do?" Dylan spat the words at Virginia, fury in her eyes as she cradled Marney.

Virginia's head spun, her ears ringing, and she gripped the nearest parked car to keep herself upright, her knees giving out beneath her.

An ambulance came and took Marney away. Virginia watched them load her onto a stretcher and roll her into the back of the ambulance, then slam the doors shut and speed off, sirens blaring. Before the ambulance was out of sight, Dylan was at Virginia's side.

"You are never to involve her in something like this again." Virginia turned to see Dylan looking at her with swollen red eyes. Her jaw was set firmly and she had a crazed look about her. "You will be nothing but support-ive. You will tell her you're happy for her, glad she's building a life at Breeze Village, and you will leave her alone."

"Dylan, I—" Virginia started to protest, but Dylan cut her off.

"No. You could have gotten her killed today. I don't want to hear it."

Dylan turned and walked away, her footsteps echoing in the absence of sirens, and Virginia wiped tears from her cheeks. Before Dylan could climb back into the unmarked police van, Virginia raised her voice and asked, "What happens now? With Matt?" She hated herself for asking it, but she also knew she'd put her best friend's life in harm's way trying to take him down, and she couldn't let that be in vain.

Disgust broke out over Dylan's face. "He's gone. We were moments away from taking him down, and the rest of his gang, too, but now he'll go to ground and we'll be back at square one."

"Gang?"

"Yes, gang. Those other three cars that were in front of the warehouse?" She shook her head. "We've been chasing them for drug and arms dealing for ages, and we were finally close to bagging them."

Virginia furrowed her brow, trying to understand. "What about the murders?"

Dylan threw her hands up in the air and barked out an angry laugh. "You really can't let go of your wild theories about Matt, can you? I told you he wasn't a suspect."

"But how…?"

"The night of Ruth's death, I was sitting in that van right there watching Matt make a deal with a known dealer from Chicago." She pointed at the van she'd emerged from minutes before. Spit flew from her mouth as she raised her voice, her anger growing. "The night of Genie's and Byron's deaths, he was in police custody being questioned. Unfortunately, we didn't have enough to keep him, and now he'll try his hardest to make sure we never do. He's a criminal and a menace, but he didn't kill anyone at Breeze Village."

back at Marney's sleeping face. "She has a concussion, and she'll probably need to stay here a few days, but we don't expect any long-term effects."

Marney's head was bandaged where she'd hit it on the sidewalk after fainting, and her curly gray hair poked out from under the wrap every which way. Traces of mascara and lipstick remained on her face, and her manicured hand was soft in Virginia's. As she held her friend's hand and watched her sleep, it struck Virginia how fragile Marney looked. Her skin was thin and translucent, dotted with age spots, and it hung looser on her slight frame than Virginia remembered.

This is all my fault. The weight of Virginia's guilt overwhelmed her. *I dragged her to follow Matt. I brought her in on this stupid investigation. I didn't let her have the peaceful next chapter in life that she wanted.*

The nurse bustled around the room, checking the tubes and machines connected to Marney, and Virginia stood to avoid feeling in the way. She gave Marney's hand one more squeeze before leaving the room.

Outside in the hallway, Virginia reached into her bag and pulled out her phone. No missed calls, no voicemails. Dylan must not have told Lawrence or her kids what was going on. Or if she had, they were too upset with her to even want to call and berate her.

She took a deep breath before dialing Lucy's number. She counted the rings before Lucy picked up, willing herself not to hang up. Willing herself to do the hard thing. The right thing.

"Mom?" Lucy sounded surprised and worried when she answered the phone. "What's going on?"

"I'm okay," Virginia reassured her. "But I need your help."

"What happened?" Virginia could hear Lucy shuffling around on the other end of the line, then the jangle of her picking up her keys.

"Not right this minute," she said. "Can you and Jack come over tomorrow morning?"

"Of course. Are you going to tell me what's going on or make us wait until morning?"

Virginia sighed. If she told Lucy Marney was in the hospital, she knew Lucy would be there in under half an hour, ready to spend the entire night beside Marney's bed. If she told her she was about to lose her house to foreclosure and was failing to fight off a shark-like developer, Lucy would be at her house maybe before Virginia could even get home.

No, Virginia thought. Her stomach growled and her eyes felt heavy. Sleep, food, and a shower, even without hot water, all vied for priority. She needed a good night's sleep, or the closest approximation she was likely to get that night, before she'd be ready to have the difficult conversations ahead.

"It can wait until tomorrow. Tell your brother. I'll see you both in the morning."

Virginia hung up before Lucy could protest. She gave one glance back through the tiny window into Marney's room, then willed her feet to carry her home. She walked like a zombie to her car and fell into bed still fully dressed.

* * *

Virginia was lying awake in bed when she heard a key turn in the front door and footsteps shuffle through the dining room and into her cramped kitchen.

"Mom?" Jack called out for her, and she could hear Lucy and Stephanie shush him.

"Just a minute." Virginia rolled onto her side and hoisted herself up, arms protesting under her own weight. Had it always been this hard to get out of bed? Was this new? She shook her head and told herself it was just the stress taking its toll, then slid her feet into her slippers and plodded to the bathroom before joining her children in the kitchen.

"We brought breakfast," Stephanie said when Virginia entered the room, rubbing her eyes. Stephanie's clothes were splattered with paint, and Virginia wondered if she'd been up all night painting or if she'd risen in the dark to get an early start.

"You guys beat the sun." Virginia accepted the coffee Stephanie offered her, avoiding her children's worried looks.

"Are you going to tell us what's going on?" Lucy gave her mother an exasperated look. "And why is the house dark?"

Virginia sighed. "I forgot to pay the electric bill."

"You what?"

Both Jack and Lucy immediately flew into a "fix it" tizzy, with Jack dialing the number for the electric company before Virginia could even take a breath.

"I've got it taken care of," Virginia said instinctively, snatching his phone away. Stephanie shot her a disappointed look, and Virginia mumbled a soft apology before handing the phone back. "Okay," she admitted. "I don't have it taken care of. But that's not what I asked you here to help me with."

"What's going on?" Lucy asked again.

Jack, Lucy, and Stephanie all stared at Virginia with a mix of anticipation and worry.

She steadied herself with the counter, taking another sip of coffee before responding in a shaky voice, "Marney is in the hospital."

"What happened?"

"Why didn't you tell us?"

"Is she going to be okay?"

Virginia held up her free hand to quiet her children so she could respond. "She has a concussion. She's going to be fine, but it's my fault she's there." The kids gaped at her in confusion. "I dragged her into a dangerous situation and things went south. She fainted and hit her head on the sidewalk."

"What kind of dangerous situation?"

"Confronting a murderer," Virginia said.

Her children's eyes widened and their jaws dropped.

"Is this about the Breeze Village murders?" Jack asked.

Virginia nodded. She cleared her throat and then came clean to her children. She told them how she'd fallen behind on her property taxes and was going to lose the house, that when Ruth turned up dead, Dorothea told her about Crime Stoppers and the potential reward money for solving a crime.

"The police just dismissed me time and time again when I brought up the things I noticed, and eventually I decided I could take it on myself, get justice for a woman who deserved better than the police were doing for her, and use the money to pay the back taxes and avoid losing the house."

For a moment, no one said anything. Without the sound of the air conditioner running, the home was completely silent.

Then, as she expected him to, Jack jumped in with solutions. "As long as Marney is going to be okay, everything else is fixable." He immediately began flipping through his phone contacts, brainstorming which of his corporate contacts might be able to help.

While he did that, Lucy walked over to her mom and wrapped Virginia in a hug. "It's going to be okay," she whispered.

Virginia sniffled and bit her tongue, trying to keep from crying. "That's not everything."

All eyes were on her again as she told them about Chelsea and how Bellemeade had bought up the entire neighborhood. "Even if I don't lose the house to my own forgetfulness with the taxes, pretty soon it'll be surrounded by construction and the property value will tank. And I've blown every chance at negotiating a fair offer from them."

Jack's mouth curled down into a frown and his brows furrowed. Virginia could practically see his wheels turning as he brainstormed their path forward.

"And I can't even move into Breeze Village," Virginia said, fully crying now. "Even if I wanted to, there's a waitlist. Oh, and I'm banned from the premises!" Her crying mixed with a twisted laugh and she knew she sounded hysterical. Jack and Lucy looked frightened, while

Stephanie cracked a smile and moved to touch Virginia's arm lovingly.

"We're the ones who should be crying if you're going to move into Breeze Village. That place is expensive!"

Jack kicked Stephanie's foot softly and gave her an admonishing look.

She giggled. "Well, it is!" Then, with a straight face, she turned back to Virginia and said, "To be clear, I was joking. Look, my nephew works for Bellemeade. I'll give him a call. And Jack will take care of the tax lien, and if Breeze Village is where you want to be, we'll find a way to make that happen, too."

But Virginia hardly heard a word Stephanie was saying. Her joke still rang in Virginia's ears. She stared out the window into the dark morning, the wheels turning, then set her coffee cup down on the counter so hard coffee splashed out and onto the linoleum.

"Sorry," she called out behind her, already slipping out of her slippers and into a pair of sneakers. "I've got to go!"

Behind her, her children were stunned.

"I really was joking," Stephanie said, her face pale. "I didn't mean anything by it."

Virginia looked at her daughter-in-law and cupped her face with a tender hand. "Thank you. Now, I've got to go settle this for good."

"What are you talking about, Mom?" Jack's voice was angry. He stood in the doorway, cell phone still in his hand, looking at Virginia as if she'd lost her mind. "You got yourself—and Marney, by the way—into this mess trying to fix all your problems yourself. Then you call us in tears to ask for our help before running off to try to fix things on your own again? Are you even listening to yourself?"

Virginia flinched at the sting of his words. "You're right." Jack's eyes widened in surprise at her admission. "I do need your help. But first, there's someone else whose help I need, if she'll forgive me."

* * *

VIRGINIA DIALED Dylan's number while driving to Matt's house. She swerved dangerously as she looked down at the keypad, and she was grateful no one else was on the road in the early morning hour. She squinted at the road signs as she passed them while listening to the phone ringing in her ear.

"What do you want?" Virginia had expected her call to wake Dylan up, but instead of sounding groggy or disoriented, Dylan sounded wide awake and impatient.

"I know who the killer is. I need you to meet me at Matt's house."

Virginia could hear Dylan let out an exasperated breath on the other end of the line. "Not this again."

"Dylan, please," Virginia started, but Dylan cut her off.

"No. I'm done with this. I'm done with you." Dylan hung up, and Virginia was once again fully alone in the car, the sound of the engine humming in the quiet morning her only companion.

Matt's street was dark. A streetlight was out, and the parked cars, trees, and hydrants all took on a ghostly appearance in its absence. The beautiful plants Ruth and, more recently, Matt, had so painstakingly curated swayed in the gentle breeze and threw shadows that looked like monsters.

Virginia looked up and down the street. Lights were off in most of the houses on the block, save for one: the one right in front of her. Matt's house.

Heart pounding in her chest, Virginia crossed the street and approached the front porch steps. Something brushed against her ankles and Virginia jumped and clapped a hand over her mouth to avoid screaming and alerting the whole street to her presence. At her feet, the small tabby cat she'd seen when the Garden Review Society visited flopped down and rolled over on its back, flashing her its belly.

"You can't scare people like that," Virginia whispered. She bent over, one hand on her thigh to support her and the other hand gently stroking the cat's soft, spotted underside.

Virginia turned her attention back to the house in front of her and slowly ascended the porch stairs. The top stair creaked under her weight, and she froze, waiting for Matt or Christine to barrel through the front door and threaten her. Instead, silence filled the air, interrupted only by the thudding of Virginia's heart in her chest, and when she was satisfied she hadn't been heard, she continued across the porch to the front door and peered inside the glass window.

Inside the house, lights shone from every room. Through the window in the front door, Virginia could see into the living room, though the view was distorted through the textured glass. She squinted through the two other windows that looked out onto the front porch. One looked into the dining room, in which nothing caught Virginia's eye, but the other looked into a bedroom where Virginia noticed drawers hanging out of the dresser and clothes spilling out onto the floor.

Virginia's stomach sank, and she hurried back over to the front door, this time ringing the doorbell. As expected, there was no answer, and when she tried the handle, the door swung open easily.

"Matt? Christine?" Virginia stepped into the living room and looked around. A flash of motion in her periphery startled Virginia, but when she turned, she saw that the cat had followed her inside and was settling itself on the sofa. "I don't think anyone is here to tell you that you can't be on the couch anymore," she said, giving the cat a pat on the head before wandering down the small hallway that led to the bedrooms.

The master bedroom told a story of someone leaving in a hurry. Drawers hung from the dresser, out-of-season tank tops and shorts littering the floor. Fancy dresses and suits still hung in the closet, and as Virginia flipped through them, a piece of pale blue fabric stuffed in the back of the closet caught her eye. She reached down and tugged on it. When she freed the fabric and saw what it was, the blood drained from her face.

In her hands, she held a wrinkled pair of blood-stained scrubs.

Though she'd felt confident Christine had murdered the Breeze Village residents, holding the bloody scrubs in her hand made it feel real and concrete. She choked on a sob, dropped the scrubs, and pulled out her phone to call Dylan again. With concrete evidence in hand, Virginia felt like she finally stood a chance at being listened to. Instead, the phone rang and rang.

After twelve rings, Virginia cursed and hung up the phone. She looked around her, trying to figure out what to do. She needed to get the police there as quickly as possible if they wanted to stand a chance at finding Matt and Christine before they were long gone.

Hand shaking, Virginia dialed 9-1-1. When the operator answered and asked what her emergency was, Virginia told her she'd gone to visit her nephew but found drugs and guns lying around and suspected he was involved in a local gang. The operator asked for her name, but Virginia just gave the woman Matt's address and hung up the phone. She prayed Dylan would be sent out to investigate, that she and her team would arrive soon.

While she waited, Virginia poked around in the bathroom and kitchen. She found a stethoscope under the bathroom sink but nothing else noteworthy.

When Dylan came barging into the house, Virginia had finished her search and was sitting on the couch petting the cat, trying to block out images of Christine drugging Ruth or bludgeoning Genie and Byron. She wasn't sure how much longer she could stand being in the house.

"What the hell is going on here?" Dylan demanded, hands on her hips. "I can have you arrested for false reporting, for misusing police resources."

Startled, the cat bolted, and Virginia stood to face Dylan.

"The killer wasn't Matt," Virginia said. "It was Christine."

She'd expected Dylan to hear her out immediately, to congratulate her on putting the puzzle pieces together.

Instead, Dylan threw her hands up in the air and shouted, "Unbelievable!"

"The bloody scrubs are in the bedroom," Virginia responded. "I imagine tests will confirm the blood belongs to Genie and Byron."

Dylan stiffened at the mention of hard evidence, and she and another officer went to the bedroom and bagged the blood-stained clothes. Dylan and her team began to put together a plan to search for Christine in Seaview, but Virginia interrupted.

"Where is Christine from, do you know? She mentioned returning to her hometown when I talked with her before."

Dylan gave Virginia a look of surprise and disapproval for having talked with Christine before, but immediately got on the radio and requested that all flights to Chicago from the nearest airport be delayed as part of an active manhunt. Virginia could see a glint of hope and excitement in Dylan's eyes despite the look of condemnation. They had their killer. Now they just needed to catch her.

Dylan and Virginia pulled into the airport in a squad car, lights and sirens blaring. Six other squad cars followed, and Virginia watched in awe as the team of uniformed officers swarmed the airport. Airport security had been alerted and was expecting them, and Dylan flashed her badge and walked off to speak in hushed voices with several stern-faced officers. They leaned over a computer, eyes narrowed as they scanned the screen, and when Dylan finally returned to Virginia, she looked angry.

"They're not here," she spat. "No passengers by their names. My guys are turning this place upside down, but so far there's no one matching their descriptions."

Virginia's heart sank. Where else could they have gone? "Could they have driven? Can you set up traffic stops or something?"

"You think I haven't already thought of that?" Dylan fumed.

Standing in the airport, nervous travelers eyeing them,

Virginia felt more defeated than she had since the start of the investigation. They'd been so close, and yet Christine had slipped right through their fingers.

"If they didn't fly, and if traffic stops haven't turned up anything, maybe they went by train? Or what about by boat?"

"You're asking me to put traffic stops around all the possible ways out of town, get my guys on every bus and train station in the area, and while we're at it, maybe get a few helicopters over the water to check for suspicious boating activity?" Dylan's voice raised as she spoke. "Do you think small-town Seaview Police has unlimited resources? We don't even know what time they left. They could be halfway to Chicago by now."

Virginia stood quietly, the scolding from Dylan building on the guilt for not putting the pieces together sooner. They were standing outside the airport now, the sunrise over the runway stunning, and in the distance, a small plane buzzed by, giving sunrise tours of the marsh to tourists.

"I've got an idea," Virginia said, hope reigniting in her gut. She pulled out her phone and dialed her friend. "Lawrence?" she said into the receiver. "I need your help."

* * *

"Why are you awake at this hour?" Lawrence asked, his sleepy voice low and gravelly over the phone.

"The kids came over this morning. I asked them to come over to help me."

This perked Lawrence up. "You asked them to come

over? To help you? Are you okay?" He sounded equal parts amazed and terrified at what Virginia's calling her children for help might signal.

"No, but you already know most of it. I assume someone told you my recklessness landed Marney in the hospital with a concussion?" Lawrence grunted an affirmative but said nothing, so Virginia continued. "I figured out who killed the Breeze Village residents, but I need your help to catch her."

Lawrence sighed on the other end of the line. "Virginia…"

"Please," Virginia begged. "This person killed Byron. To catch them would mean a lot to Marney and will probably also mean a promotion for Dylan at work after all the trouble I've caused her."

"I don't know how I could possibly be of help."

Virginia's voice caught in her throat as she thought about what she was asking of Lawrence. "I need you to reach out to Ben's old pilot buddies." She hadn't spoken the name of Lawrence's late partner in over a decade.

"Virginia, I can't do that." Lawrence's voice sounded broken on the other end, and she knew he was biting back tears.

"I know it's horrible of me to ask you for this. You've given me more help in my life than a person has a right to ask for, and instead of thanking you, I haven't even acknowledged it because I never wanted to need help. But right now, I do need your help. And Dylan needs your help."

"Dylan's still talking to you after yesterday?"

"She wasn't, but now she is." Virginia glanced over and

forth, feeling useless. She kept her phone in her hand, peeking at it several times a minute to make sure she hadn't missed a message from Lawrence. The only messages she'd received so far were from her kids wanting to make sure she was safe.

Oh, I'm safe all right. Nowhere near the murderous bitch. Her impatience turned to anger as the sun rose in the sky and more people began bustling around the airport. Wasn't there anything more they could be doing?

Before she could bring about Dylan's wrath by asking her yet again what more they could do, the phone rang in Virginia's hand. "It's Lawrence!" she shouted, nearly dropping the phone onto the concrete in her excitement.

"Hello?" The brief seconds waiting for Lawrence to speak were the longest of Virginia's life.

"I got something," he finally said, and Virginia's stomach flipped with excitement. "One of Ben's old buddies gave the couple a tour a few days ago, and then this morning they paid him cash to take them to Atlanta."

"Atlanta?" Virginia said in surprise.

Dylan got on the phone with the station to relay every bit of information Lawrence gave them.

"They said the tour was so lovely they wanted to enjoy that feeling again, and they had to go to Atlanta for a wedding. I'm guessing there's no wedding, and they just wanted to avoid the local airports?"

Virginia turned to see that Dylan's face had gone pale. "Make sure that flight doesn't get off the ground!" she yelled into her own phone before hanging up. "How quickly could Lawrence's friend get us to Atlanta?"

CHAPTER 29

Virginia had never been in a small plane before. She'd only flown three times in her life, every one of them for conferences where Earl was presenting his work. She felt butterflies in her stomach as she donned the headphones and let Michael, the pilot, and Dylan help her up into the small aircraft. She wasn't sure whether the butterflies were excitement at being on the brink of taking down a killer or nerves at the prospect of flying in a tiny tin can with a pilot in his seventies. Upon takeoff, the answer made itself clear: it was nerves.

After peering out the window and then having to work to hold herself back from vomiting, Virginia kept her eyes focused down on her lap and concentrated on her breathing. The small plane jostled and lurched, but as they passed over a large lake, the ride smoothed out and Virginia risked a glance outside. It was beautiful. Colorful blooms covered the trees surrounding the lake, and she could see the boats of early morning fishermen crossing the water.

By the time they neared Atlanta, Virginia was peering out the window with wide eyes like a child seeing Disney World for the first time. Her stomach had calmed, and she was able to appreciate the skyline as they approached.

Up front, Michael communicated with the tower over the radio. They'd had to receive special permission to enter the airspace around such a large airport, and when they were finally cleared to land he called out, "Hold on tight, ladies!"

Virginia did as she was told, gripping the seat beneath her so hard her knuckles turned white, and Michael let out a laugh.

When the wheels touched the runway, Virginia let out a sigh of relief, and as they turned from the runway onto a taxiway, they were greeted by half a dozen Atlanta PD cars. One of the officers approached the door of their plane as soon as Michael had powered off the engine. He offered Dylan a hand, and when she had hopped down out of the plane he turned and looked Virginia up and down.

"Why'd you bring Grandma along?" he asked with a smirk.

"This is Virginia Walker," Dylan said sharply, offering Virginia her hand and working with Michael to help Virginia out of the back of the plane while the officer stood off to the side. "She's an incredibly valuable piece of this investigation, and I'd appreciate it if you'd treat her as such."

Virginia's chest swelled with pride and her face flushed. She knew she wasn't forgiven for the harm she'd caused, but for Dylan to acknowledge her contribution to the investigation was huge. She hoped it was a sign that she could repair their relationship in time.

The officer grumbled a response and then introduced himself to Dylan as Captain Darby.

"Where's our plane?" Dylan asked, looking at the long line of planes lined up along the gates.

"Gate D36, on the other side of the airport."

The three piled into one of the police cars and sped with lights and sirens on full blast to the concourse in question, Virginia holding onto the seat as the car careened around a corner. As they pulled up toward their gate, they could see angry passengers disembarking the plane and being loaded onto buses.

"What the hell is going on here?" Dylan demanded of one of the staff members shuffling passengers onto buses. "Why are they deplaning?"

"We can't hold passengers on a plane on the tarmac for longer than three hours, and we'd already pulled away from the gate when we got the hold orders. By law, we have to unload them and bring them back to the gate."

Dylan began to argue with the attendant, their loud voices joining the chorus of frustrated passengers being herded from one cramped vehicle to another. Curses and jabs flew from the lips of the angry travelers as they bumped into one another, each eager to stretch their legs, even if it was just a few steps between the plane and the bus.

Virginia watched the bumbling crowd, feeling grateful not to be part of it, when suddenly a flash of brunette hair caught her eye. There, heads down, were Christine and Matt, trying to hurry from the plane to the bus. Pulling up with a half dozen cop cars wasn't exactly a stealth move, and Virginia saw Christine pulling Matt along as he looked around, confused. She wondered how much he knew about her motives for getting out of Seaview.

"There!" she shouted, pointing at them. Christine's gaze snapped to Virginia and they made eye contact, a mix of surprise and hatred on Christine's face.

"Come on," Christine said to Matt, yanking his arm as she took off at a run. Before she could get five steps away from the rest of the crowd, a man in a suit tackled her to the ground, and Matt stopped, stunned. He looked from Virginia to his wife on the concrete, then turned on his heel to try to run but was stopped by a middle-aged woman with a baby strapped to her chest standing square in his way.

"I don't think so," she told him. Her baby let out a squeal and Matt recoiled, a look of disgust on his face.

"Thanks for your help," Dylan said to Virginia with a grin as she slapped handcuffs on both Matt and Christine. "Without your persistence, a murderer would have walked free today."

"Whoa, whoa, whoa," Matt said, panic spreading across his face. "I never killed anyone!"

"Maybe you didn't—unless you count the deaths associated with the drugs and guns you've pumped into our community—but your wife certainly did." Virginia stepped forward and put her hands on her hips, feeling powerful.

Matt's eyes grew wide, and his jaw dropped as he looked from Virginia to where Dylan stood over Christine. "My own mother?" His voice quavered with disbelief, and Virginia saw a tear spring from his eye and roll down his cheek.

* * *

"Chrissy, tell me you didn't." Matt's voice was pleading as he looked at his wife.

"I don't know what they're talking about," she said, but her hesitation gave her away.

"Oh, you know what I'm talking about," Virginia said, stepping forward. "You put on a pair of scrubs and made yourself look like you worked at Breeze Village. You snuck in and slipped into Ruth's room, where you poisoned her. You knew she was on blood thinners, so you dissolved them in her tea, thinking everyone would figure she'd just taken too many, forgetful in her old age."

Matt was aghast, staring open-mouthed at Christine.

"What I haven't managed to put together yet, and maybe you can help me here, is why Genie had to go. Byron, I believe, was in the wrong place at the wrong time, but Genie? Did she just know too much?"

Christine sputtered, unable to deny the accusations being levied against her.

"She was in business with your husband, wasn't she? She faked prescriptions to get her hands on a boatload of painkillers; he peddled them on the streets. Am I right?" She looked to Matt and he nodded, not even trying to deny it. His eyes drooped and his jaw hung slack. He looked like a broken man.

"Genie also sold pot for me in the nursing home," he

said, looking at the ground. "Turns out, old people with chronic pain are a good market."

"So why kill her?" Virginia asked again, staring into Christine's dark eyes. "She was profitable, no?"

"You were never going to leave Seaview!" Christine said, trying to look up at Matt though she was still lying facedown on the ground in handcuffs. "I thought you'd be excited to leave once your mother was out of the picture. She's the whole reason we moved to this stupid town in the first place! Then she finally kicks the bucket and we're free to move on with our lives, but no, you're in too deep, the money's too good, the timing's not right." Tears fell from her own eyes as she shouted.

Christine's voice lowered and took on a venomous tone. "You owed me. You promised me. We had a good life. I had a good life. It was your fault we had to leave the city, your gambling debts that forced me to close my restaurant and rely on your mother for support." She spat the words. "I thought you'd be happy we'd finally be able to get out of here. With the inheritance money, we could go anywhere, do anything!"

"You thought I'd be happy you killed my mother?" Matt bellowed with such force he lost his balance with his hands cuffed behind his back and nearly fell over. The close call seemed to bring him back into his body and he looked around as if only then realizing where he was, that there was a crowd of onlookers watching with a mixture of horror and glee.

"Get them out of here," Dylan said to Captain Darby. He and his officers obliged, shoving Matt and Christine into the back of a squad car and driving off.

"Sorry we ruined your flight," Virginia said to the crowd of passengers. Instead of anger, the group erupted in applause.

Virginia felt pride well up inside her and a grin spread across her face. She'd done it.

CHAPTER 30

"Tell me again about the lady with the baby just stepping right in Matt's path." Marney beamed up at Virginia from her hospital bed, eyes twinkling. It was Sunday morning, and though Virginia had arrived before seven, Marney still gave her a hard time for not coming straight to the hospital when they'd gotten back from Atlanta the previous day.

When Virginia described Matt's face when the baby squealed at him, Marney roared with laughter, her chest rising and falling, head thrown back against her pillow. She still wore a bandage around her head, but she looked much better than she had when Virginia had seen her thirty-six hours before. When Marney's laughter died down, she looked at Virginia with love in her eyes and Virginia took her hand.

"I am so sorry," she said, her voice cracking.

"I know you are." Marney put her hand on top of Virginia's, forming a little stack as if they were children playing a game at recess.

"I shouldn't have dragged you along. I shouldn't have gone in the first place."

"You know I'd never let you go alone," Marney said, a mischievous smile spreading across her face, "but I'll accept your admission that you shouldn't have gone chasing Matt."

"Although if they'd brought him in on drug and arms dealing, we'd never have gotten Christine for murder. I only figured it out thanks to a joke Stephanie made about crying over paying for a mother-in-law to be in Breeze Village."

Marney cocked her head to the side, considering this, but said nothing.

"There is something else I wanted to tell you," Virginia said. Marney sat up with anticipation. "I've put myself on the waitlist for Breeze Village."

"We're going to be neighbors again?" Marney's face lit up with excitement and she pulled Virginia down to hug her.

"Eventually. I wish health, happiness, and longevity to all the residents of Breeze Village, but I admit part of me would like a room to open up sooner rather than later. I'm staying with my kids until there's a spot for me."

Marney gasped. "You're not serious!" Virginia nodded and Marney clapped her hands over her mouth. "Which one?"

"I'll be alternating, a week at a time at each of their places. Maybe Lawrence will let me spend a week at his swanky new beachside condo sometime, too."

Marney's brow knit together. "So, does this mean you've accepted an offer with that developer?"

"The kids are handling that for me. It's actually a bit of a long story. Jack is actually helping me take care of the taxes so the government doesn't foreclose on the home, and Stephanie has a nephew at Bellemeade who is going to make sure they give me a fair offer."

"Wait, back up. Foreclosure?"

Virginia laughed. Having her family's help and support had taken a weight off her shoulders, and she finally felt like she could breathe. "I was too embarrassed to tell you. But we've all seen where that's landed me, so I'm trying a new strategy of asking for help. So far, it's great."

Marney squeezed Virginia's hand and the two shared a laugh.

"I do have one question for you. Are cats allowed at Breeze Village?" Without waiting for a response, Virginia picked up her bag and pulled out the tiny tabby cat who had lived outside Matt's house, looking around to make sure no nurses were nearby. "This little guy is going to need a new home."

Virginia set the cat on Marney's lap and he immediately began kneading the blanket and purring contentedly. Marney beamed with delight as she rubbed behind his ears and gave his little head a kiss.

"Does he come with a name?" she asked.

Virginia shook her head.

"What about Pancake?" Marney asked. "Or Waffle. Maybe Muffin? Can you tell they're basically starving me here?"

The door to the room swung open and Virginia and Marney both jumped, rushing to hide the cat, but looked up to see that it was only Lawrence. In his hand he held up a brown paper bag.

"I think I can help," he said with a smile.

As the three shared hash browns and breakfast sandwiches and took turns cuddling their new feline companion, Virginia felt a peace wash over her. The thought that only a few miles away her children were on the phone working out the logistics of selling her family home didn't touch her the way she expected. Yes, she was sad, but sitting there with her two closest friends, Virginia felt at home. She even felt an inkling of anticipation at moving into Breeze Village. After all, she had a feeling she'd never want for excitement there.

ACKNOWLEDGMENTS

This book would never have seen the light of day without the support of so many. Thank you to my parents for encouraging me to write. Thank you for every time you asked me, "How's your book going?" It pushed me to actually finish it. Thank you to my brother, Andrew, for letting me borrow your middle name. Thank you to Ken, the best partner a person could have. Thank you for setting the early alarms so I could write in the mornings. Thank you for putting the kettle on so the water is already hot by the time I get downstairs. Thank you for your enthusiastic support of this dream of mine. My baby is the best baby. Thank you to Theo, our sweet boy, for the snuggles and for all the "help" every time I sat down to write. Thank you, Molly, the biscuit to my cabbage, for loving me and this idea. Your profound impact on me and my life goes so much further than this book, but it (and its predecessors, my NaNoWriMo babies) would never have existed without you. Finally, thank you to the 20Books-

To50K Facebook group and the thousands of indie authors who make that group the phenomenal source of inspiration and knowledge that it is. A rising tide lifts all boats.

"Not much," the pile seemed to say, staring back at her.

The attic produced similarly discouraging results: plastic tubs of the kids' old stuffed animals and baby clothes, the two lamps that had previously occupied the buffet table, and a half dozen of Earl's old instruments. She could never part with the guitars and saxophone. He'd played those almost daily, serenading her as she dressed in the mornings, impressing their friends after warm dinner parties. So she picked up a dusty trumpet case instead and carried it downstairs, her slippered feet moving slowly down the small, steep staircase.

Back on solid ground, no longer having to hunch over, Virginia popped the latch on the case and opened it up to reveal a silver trumpet Earl had played only a handful of times in all the years they'd been together. It had been a gift, but it had spent more time on display than being used, and when the cancer won its battle, Virginia had put it back in its case and hadn't looked at it since.

No longer able to bite back the tears, Virginia wiped her face, shut the instrument case, and stood. There might not be a market for old handbags, but surely an instrument like this would still have some value. Her vision blurred by tears, Virginia started down the hall before her foot connected with something solid. The trumpet case fell from her hand, and she reached out to catch herself before landing hard on the wooden floor. Intense pain shot from her wrist up her arm, and Virginia cradled it in her other arm while she assessed her situation.

Other than the hurt wrist, she seemed fine. Her leg would bruise, she was sure of it, but she hadn't hit her head.

leg up on the rest of the neighborhood. She dialed Kim Nguyen's number and waited as it rang.

"Virginia!" Kim greeted her with enthusiasm, bringing a small smile back to Virginia's face.

"Kim, you won't believe what I've just heard." Legitimate excitement bubbled up in Virginia. She paused a moment for dramatic effect. "Marney Richards is moving to Breeze Village."

"I thought I'd heard that," Kim said, and the excitement vanished from Virginia's body as quickly as it had appeared. "Sometime soon, right?"

"Tomorrow," Virginia confirmed. Her stomach sank in disbelief that Kim knew about Marney's move before she did.

"Wow, that's sooner than I'd expected! Rumors have been flying, and at first, I said, 'No, you've got to have heard wrong, Marney Richards has lived in Grove Park for decades, there's no way she's moving,' but then Sue and Dorothea heard the rumors, too. When Julia from the hairdresser's reached out to me and said she'd heard it, then I knew it had to be true. What I'm so surprised about, Virginia, is that you kept it quiet all this time!"

Virginia mustered the closest thing to a laugh as she could. "Well, I *can* keep a secret."

"For a while," Kim joked. "You did eventually call to tell me."

"Well, when the secret is this juicy, I guess there's a limit to how long I can keep it inside."

"You say she's moving tomorrow? I've got to give Dorothea a call. She was trying to tell me Marney was moving next month. I'll have to let her know her source large computer hummed as if already exhausted. "Have a seat," Dr. DiMarco said before pulling up a chair for himself. "We're pretty low tech around here. We keep paper files on all our patients, but I've been moving toward using an automated scheduling system."

Virginia's eyes darted to the computer and her throat tightened. She had never warmed up to the latest technology.

"The most important things I need from you are to take calls, schedule appointments, and pull patient files for me before appointments to reduce the downtime in between patients."

Take calls and schedule appointments. I can do that.

Virginia's phone rang in her bag and she jumped. "I am so sorry." As she dug in her purse for the phone, the ringtone seemed louder and louder, and she could feel Dr. DiMarco's gaze on her. When she finally pulled the phone from the bag and declined the call—*what does Lucy want this morning?*—the silence felt deafening.

"Everything okay?" Dr. DiMarco asked, and Virginia nodded, tucking the phone back into her bag.

Dr. DiMarco guided Virginia through the file systems on the computer, and she pulled out a notepad and took detailed notes as he talked. She prayed the note-taking came across as dedication and not a dead giveaway that her memory wasn't what it had once been.

As Dr. DiMarco turned one of the large black wheels on the side of a row of shelves, rolling the accordion unit out to expose a new block of file folders, Virginia's phone rang again, startling them both.

Matt staggered back a step. "What are you talking about?"

"They're saying she took too many of her blood thinners, but by the looks of her medicine cabinet, she'd never mistime a dose of anything."

Matt frowned and shook his head. "I think you should get out of here."

"No one is asking questions or looking into this at all. Ruth deserves answers."

"My mother deserves peace." Matt exhaled sharply. "Not wannabe detectives sticking their noses where they don't belong."

He stared down at Virginia until she held up her hands in surrender and stepped out of Ruth's room and into the hallway. She ducked into the hall bathroom but waited by the door until she heard his footsteps walking past. When the footsteps had faded, she pulled open the door and walked down the hall after him. Through the dining room, she could see out onto the courtyard; he wasn't there. She crossed the lobby, and through the window to the parking lot, she saw him stepping into a small white Mazda and speeding away.

What are you up to?

* * *

AFTER MATT'S Mazda turned a corner and drifted out of sight, Virginia remained by the window, watching the moss hanging down from the ancient oaks drifting in the wind until Marney's voice stirred her from her thoughts.

"Where did you get off to?"

Breeze Village. She seemed as young and spry as any of us."

"She's actually in one of their independent living cottages," Virginia said. "So she doesn't have nurses coming to check up on her or anything, but she has access to the amenities and no more yardwork or worrying with home repairs." She stared down at her plate, wanting to change the subject but not knowing how.

"I heard someone died there just the other day," the woman in the center of the sofa said.

The rest of the women gasped and turned to look at her.

"Now, Jan, let's not talk about such unpleasant things." Kim sipped her tea with a look of distaste.

"The gardens there are really quite nice," Virginia said, turning to Gemma. "Maybe the Garden Review Society could consider them for a future edition of the *Review*."

"That's a wonderful idea, maybe on—"

"I heard it was a grizzly death," Jan continued, cutting Gemma off. Her dyed-black hair stood piled high atop her head, bouncing as she talked. "Blood everywhere."

At this, even Kim set her tea down and looked at Jan with wide, expectant eyes. "What happened?"

"Actually," Virginia said, shooting Jan a frown, "it wasn't a grizzly death at all. The woman had a stroke. No blood, no gore." The women looked at her quizzically, and Virginia added, "I found her, so I would know."

"No! You found her?" Dorothea's bracelets jangled as she threw her hands up in front of her mouth.

Virginia nodded solemnly. "From what I've heard, the official statement is that she took too many of her blood

that the more people she talked with who might have known Ruth, the better.

COLLEEN'S ROOM was on the third floor of the main building at Breeze Village. It would have overlooked the church across the street from the building had the windows not been covered in gauzy maroon-colored fabric. Crystals occupied nearly every flat surface and sparkly beaded strings hung from the ceiling. On a low coffee table sat a crystal ball, and Virginia counted four decks of tarot cards. Colleen lit a stick of incense and set it on the table.

"Sit, sit," she said, gesturing for Marney and Virginia to sit on a small loveseat and pulling up a chair across the table from them. They did as they were told, and Virginia was surprised how far she sank down into the soft, worn leather when she sat. She wondered if she'd be able to get back up on her own. "What brings you to me this fine morning?"

"You don't know? I thought you were a psychic," Virginia said.

Colleen frowned. "I have connections to the spirit world. Visions come to me. But I am not a mind reader, nor do I have visions of every event that is to take place. Were I to hold that much inside my mind, I do believe it might kill me."

Marney cleared her throat to respond. "My apologies for my friend, Colleen. She's the unfortunate one who found Ruth Beaumont dead in her room, and she's been the table Virginia noticed a tremor. He moved his hand to his lap and cleared his throat.

"Of course. I'm so glad she's found such kind people to make her transition to Breeze Village easier."

"I'm just glad she decided now was the right time to make a big life change." He looked over to Marney, and Virginia felt a pang. He looked at Marney the way Earl had looked at her when they first started dating, like he adored her.

"Oh, there's Lawrence," Marney said, holding up her hand and waving at their friend.

Virginia felt her stomach sink, and Lawrence gave her a piercing stare as he crossed the restaurant floor to join them in their booth.

"I didn't know you were joining us," Virginia said.

"When you called and asked what our lunch plans were yesterday, I gave Lawrence a call to see if he could join us." Marney seemed delighted to have both her friends here to meet Byron.

Virginia wanted to dissolve into the floor.

A waitress with a teal mohawk came to take their order, and while they sipped drinks and waited for their food to arrive, Byron said, "You know, my coworkers and I used to come here every Friday for lunch. Back when it was Johnny C's Pizza Parlor. They had the best mojitos in town."

"You were an attorney, right?" Virginia asked.

Lawrence gave her a warning look, silently commanding her not to turn this into an interrogation. Virginia ignored him, keeping her gaze on Byron.

Byron nodded. "I was. I ended up in criminal defense,

breathing. She wondered how many of the residents could take the stairs if there were an emergency or the elevator was down for maintenance. By law, it was a requirement that any resident assigned a room on an upper floor be physically capable of using the stairs, but while Virginia could technically use the stairs, she contemplated the likelihood of outpacing a fire if she were faced with the need.

The outside of Colleen's door was decorated with a curtain of sparkling beads depicting the lunar phases. Virginia took a deep breath and knocked twice. The door opened almost immediately, the beads clattering as the door swung back to reveal Colleen standing in a dark blue velvet robe and wearing a knowing smile.

"I wondered when you would return," she said, beckoning Virginia inside. "What brings you here this evening?"

"You're the psychic. You knew I'd return but didn't know why?" Virginia was instantly irritated with Colleen and her all-knowing smile. She took a deep breath and tried to calm herself, offering an apology while Colleen brushed it off, the smile not wavering.

"You seem shaken. Would you like a cup of tea?"

Virginia accepted the warm mug and sat down on the squishy loveseat she had shared with Marney when they'd visited before. She took care to sit on the edge to avoid sinking down so much that she wouldn't be able to get up again on her own.

"The strangest thing happened this morning," Virginia began. Her face flushed with embarrassment, and she had to coax herself to continue. "This man came to my work, until Marney rounded a corner and disappeared, then realized she had started to cry. She hastily wiped the tears from her cheeks and turned to go back inside the doctor's office and finish out her shift, but she couldn't get Marney's words out of her head. Who did she think she was, prying into everyone's lives with this investigation when she wouldn't even tell her best friends that she was working a part-time secretary job because she was dangerously close to losing her house?

No. She wasn't prying, seeking out juicy gossip. She was investigating because a woman was dead and no one was taking it seriously. Virginia went through the motions for the rest of the day, but when the time came to clock out, she felt more relief at leaving than she'd felt since her first disastrous shift.

* * *

VIRGINIA PULLED INTO HER DRIVEWAY, surprised to see a woman walking away from her front door and down the concrete pathway through her front yard. She squinted and touched her fingertips to her lips, trying to place the woman, then let out an expletive when she realized it was the property developer who had come before, trying to buy her house.

She stepped out of the car, first turning sideways and placing both feet on the driveway before using both arms to heft herself from the seat. Her mobility had long since precluded her from sliding in and out of the car gracefully, and she hoped the developer didn't see it as a sign of weakness.

after Ruth's memorial, but didn't have high hopes that this new lawman would take her seriously.

For the next fifteen minutes, Detective Kincaid questioned Virginia and Marney. He began by asking them to describe the scene they'd come upon in the hallway and why they'd been there at that moment in time. When Virginia explained that they'd been on their way to Genie's room to peek into her medicine cabinet, the detective frowned at her and asked her to elaborate.

Virginia explained that she'd found a surprising amount of pill bottles earlier and that she believed Genie was involved in something shady. Detective Kincaid continued making notes on the clipboard he held in his lap, and Virginia added that she'd seen Genie with Matt earlier that day. "I think they're involved in something together, something nefarious, and I think it might be related to Ruth's death."

To Virginia's surprise, rather than dismissing this piece of information, Detective Kincaid looked up at her with intense eyes and a furrowed brow. "That's Matt Beaumont?"

Virginia nodded, but when she and Marney asked why that was so alarming, the officer refused to tell them anything further. He made a few final notes on his clipboard before standing and offering his hand to shake theirs.

"Thank you for your time and your openness this evening."

The officer left them, and Virginia and Marney turned to each other, the exhaustion taking over now that they were alone.

That was the breaking point, and Virginia exploded. Lawrence tried to explain to her that he'd been looking at small condos closer to the beach, but Virginia cut him off, accusing him of lying, of keeping secrets, of selling his soul by making a deal with this property company.

At this, Lawrence cocked his head to the side and gave Virginia a questioning look. "Wait, you haven't?"

Virginia shook her head, and Lawrence looked almost as worried as the other neighbors had when Virginia had told them the same thing.

"I'm sorry I hadn't talked to you sooner, but I thought it was the elephant in the room that neither of us wanted to bring up. It's a tough topic."

Virginia bit back tears. "I'm not moving. This neighborhood is my home. This *house* is my home. I thought you felt the same."

Lawrence tried to protest, but Virginia ignored him as she crossed the rest of the yard and closed the front door behind her. When she was alone she let the tears fall down her face, the reality that Bellemeade was buying up the entire neighborhood hitting her. All of a sudden, it seemed she was standing alone on the Titanic trying to fight the iceberg while everyone around her had been securing lifeboats.

eyes were still swollen from crying and she'd barely slept, the image of Matt's face on a corkboard in the police station coming to her every time she closed her eyes, and Colleen's comments about the tea in Genie's room filled her ears when she stepped away from the sounds of the television.

"If that god damned developer is here again, I'm going to lose it," she muttered to herself. Virginia's joints ached as she pulled herself from the couch and hobbled to the door. When she put her face to the door and looked out the peephole, she was surprised to see Marney standing on her porch, plastic grocery bags in her hands.

"Go away!" Virginia shouted.

"Let me in," Marney answered, "or I'll use the key you gave me and let myself in."

"I'll call the cops," Virginia threatened, but she turned the lock as she said it and pulled the door open.

Marney looked at Virginia with sad eyes that begged forgiveness. "I am so sorry," she said, her voice barely more than a whisper. "I should have asked you about the house, the developer, all of it. And Lawrence, too. We shouldn't have stayed quiet. But you've got to understand—"

"I understand," Virginia cut her off. And she did. As much as it hurt to know her closest friends had known her secrets—or at least some of them—and said nothing, she knew she wouldn't have reacted well if they'd brought it up. And she was still hiding the biggest secret, the possibility that she wouldn't have a house left to sell if she didn't sort things out with the taxes. She still wasn't ready to share that with Marney or Lawrence.

of her hands and looked up to see Dylan and the man she recognized as Detective Kincaid walking toward them, accompanied by Michelle, the owner of Breeze Village.

Dylan's mouth curled down in a frown and her eyes gleamed with anger. "We need to speak with you about an alleged assault."

* * *

VIRGINIA'S STOMACH SANK. An assault. She was trying to stop a murderer in action, and now she was being charged with assault?

She wasn't being charged, Dylan clarified. At least not yet. Ronald's burns were painful but not serious. He was going to be fine, and he would rather avoid any legal unpleasantness.

Virginia let out a sigh of relief. "I didn't mean to hurt Ronald, but he was about to drink that tea. Haley is the killer. She had access to all the victims, and by taking them out, she secured a spot for her mother in Breeze Village instead of on the waitlist."

Dylan frowned. "That is a serious allegation."

Of course, it was a serious allegation. People were dead! And one more person could have died tonight if she hadn't been there. Virginia wondered how her allegations against a murderer could possibly be more serious than the murder itself.

"I can help clear this up," Haley said, approaching. "Virginia, what exactly is it you think I've done?"

Anger welled up inside Virginia. Haley batted her false eyelashes, but all Virginia could see was the image of her been such a hit. Marney had been so excited she'd been practically glowing when she'd handed Virginia the flier and asked her to come to the market to support her.

Guilt sitting like a rock in the pit of her stomach, Virginia set aside the piles of bills and statements and checked her watch. Even if she hurried, she was unlikely to make it to the market in time to take Marney's class. In her mind's eye, she could see herself hurrying over to Marney's booth as everyone left. She pictured the small frown on Marney's face as she reassured Virginia that it was all right; it hadn't been that big of a deal, anyway. But Virginia knew it was a big deal, and her friend deserved her support.

"Late is better than absent," she told herself, then picked up her purse and headed out the door.

Before climbing into her car, Virginia crouched despite her knees' protests and snipped some blooms from her garden. As she crouched, trying to hold herself steady without getting the knees of her pant legs too dirty, she glanced over at Lawrence's house and wondered if he was already at the market with Marney.

Virginia tucked the flowers into a vase and propped it up in the passenger seat of her car, then walked across the lawn to knock on Lawrence's door. No answer. She knocked two more times before giving up and returning to her car alone to head to the festival.

* * *

WHEN VIRGINIA ARRIVED at the festival, the park was bustling. Booths lined the sidewalks around the perimeter

Marney was taken to the local hospital in Seaview. Virginia was reassured by the fact that they kept her there rather than moving her to one of the larger hospitals in the bigger cities close by. Virginia's sneakers squeaked on the linoleum floors as she padded along, searching for Marney's room.

While Marney lay unconscious in her hospital bed, Virginia decorated the room with flowers from her garden, then sat and held Marney's hand. The rhythmic rise and fall of Marney's chest combined with the beeps from the machines hooked up to her lulled Virginia into a relaxed state, and for a moment she even drifted off to sleep herself. She was startled awake by the door opening, and a young black nurse with kind eyes entered the room.

"How is she?" Virginia asked, her voice pleading. "They let me in, but they wouldn't tell me anything."

"She's going to be okay." The nurse's expression was soft and her voice was soothing. Virginia felt her shoulders relax at the assurance from the nurse and cast a gaze saw Dylan scowling at her. "Only in the context of this investigation." Silence fell on the call, and Virginia grew impatient. "Will you do it?"

Another beat passed before Lawrence agreed. "What do you need from Ben's friends?" His voice cracked on Ben's name.

"I need to know whether any of them, or any of their other pilot buddies, has taken a couple on a flight, Matt and Christine Beaumont. They may have used fake names, so I'll send you a picture."

"I'll reach out to them," Lawrence said quietly, "but I can't promise they'll pick up. I haven't talked with them since Ben's funeral."

"Thank you, thank you, thank you," Virginia repeated. She wanted to remind him that this was time-sensitive, to ask him to go knock on doors and get the answers she needed, but she stopped herself.

The call disconnected, and Virginia looked over to see Dylan's expectant face.

"What's the deal?" Dylan asked her.

"We wait for a call back."

* * *

THE WAIT for Lawrence's call back felt like hours. Dylan spent the time on the phone, coordinating with her team to send officers to the train station and bus stations and to contact all airports within a three-hour drive to see whether they had a Matt or Christine Beaumont booked on any of their flights.

While Dylan was occupied, Virginia paced back and

ABOUT THE AUTHOR

A Georgia peach, Kate Maclean grew up in historic Savannah, Georgia, and spent much of her childhood reading Nancy Drew and Hercule Poirot mysteries on her backyard swing.

This lifelong lover of mysteries and crime dramas now lives outside Washington, D.C., with her partner and their cat. This is her first book.

www.ingramcontent.com/pod-product-compliance
Lightning Source LLC
Chambersburg PA
CBHW020146310726
48970CB00006B/2035